OUT IN THE SPECTRUM

ARTICLES, STORIES, AND RECIPES BY AUTISTIC ADULTS FOR AUTISTIC ADULTS

Compiled and Edited by Akosua Joy Brown

Contributors: Owen Bryan, Scott R. Dawson, Ciara Freeman, Justin Humphreys, Corey Kearns, Eric Lauder, Katherine Layne, Brianna Longhenry, Justin Milner, Elliot Smith, Wayman Edward Sole, Robert Williams

PressesRenaissancePress.ca

First edition 2025

Cover art by What's Your Story - Author Services.
Compiled and Edited by Akosua Joy Brown
Proofread by Molly Desson.

Legal deposit, Library and Archives Canada, April 2025.

Paperback ISBN: 978-1-990086-66-3
Ebook ISBN: 978-1-990086-72-4

Renaissance Press - pressesrenaissancepress.ca

Renaissance acknowledges that it is hosted on the traditional, unceded land of the Anishinabek, the Kanien'kehá:ka, and the Omàmìwininìwag. We acknowledge the privileges and comforts that colonialism has granted us and vow to use this privilege to disrupt colonialism by lifting up the voices of marginalized humans who continue to suffer the effects of ongoing colonialism.

Printed in Gatineau at
Imprimerie Gauvin
Depuis 1892
gauvin.ca

Renaissance gratefully acknowledges the support of the Canada Council for the Arts

"Here's to the crazy ones, the misfits, the rebels, the troublemakers, the round pegs in the square holes… the ones who see things differently — they're not fond of rules, and they have no respect for the status quo… Because the people who are crazy enough to think they can change the world, are the ones who do."

— Steve Jobs

TABLE OF CONTENTS

Introduction:
Embracing the Spectrum of Stories
By Akosua Brown

Though I am not autistic, I am neurodivergent, and I have some understanding of the challenge of navigating a world built for neurotypical people. For those of us who process, think, and experience differently, the mental load can be overwhelming. For people on the autism spectrum, this challenge is even greater—a system designed without them in mind creates daily hurdles that require extraordinary strength, resilience, and adaptability.

My personal connection to autism runs deep. My son was diagnosed with autism. His journey has profoundly shaped how I view the world. For a time, I ran a magazine dedicated to amplifying supporting autistic children—helping them to celebrate differences, to understand themselves. To help others accept and value diversity. Over the course of 20 issues, we created a space where teenagers on the spectrum wrote and were peer advisors for the magazine. Many of those contributors are now writers in this book, and their words are as insightful, raw, and brave as ever.

I then created a program called "Creative Expressions" for the charity Autism Home Base. Through our program we ended up creating so much material we decided to share it through radio plays, a wee movie we made, and a book. The original title of this book was *Oops! We Actually Wrote a Book in the End* as writing a book was a delightful consequence, but not the reason for the fun and connection we enjoyed through the program. However, when I invited new members to the group, the original title was no longer fitting. We chose to change the title as our new aim *was* to write this book. We called it "Out in the Spectrum" because these are stories of people on the spectrum out in the world.

This compilation is more than a collection of stories—it is a testament to the power of community. Throughout the process of creating this book, our contributors found a safe, supportive space in which to share their voices. In our meetings, we laughed, brainstormed, and bonded, building a camaraderie rooted in mutual respect and understanding. That spirit of connection shines through in the pages that follow.

You'll see we are presenting some conversations illustrated like video-conferencing meetings. Presented to show conversations as they unfolded. In doing this, we hoped to capture not only the creativity and humor of our contributors but also their bravery in sharing their perspectives. This book stands as a reminder that while the world may not always feel accommodating, there are spaces where neurodivergent voices can thrive—and this is one of them.

How To Use This Book

The book is divided into parts, and contributors wrote articles and stories for as many parts as they wanted to. You do not need to read the book in a chronological fashion—it is made to be "dip-in-able." Read stories in whichever order suits you.

You may find you want to read more about relationships, as that is something you are interested in at the moment—start there if you wish! In the independence section, we included some recipes as, cooking for yourself is one thing that most members were most proud of. We are so pleased to include their favourite dishes so you can try them yourselves.

There is a lot to enjoy in this book. Welcome to a celebration of authenticity, resilience, and the transformative power of storytelling.

PART 1:
ABOUT US

Understanding Me and The History of Autism
By Ciara Freeman

For a long time, the public perception of what autism is, and what an autistic person looks like, has been skewed by stereotypes perpetuated by doctors and scientists using out of date research. Science isn't static; it's forever changing and with each generation of new minds, our understanding on any subject deepens. Autism is no exception.

Many think the concept of autism first came about in 1943 from Leo Kanner, an Austrian-American psychiatrist and physician. Back then, it was coined as "infantile autism," a term used to describe a set of "abnormal behaviours" beginning from infancy. But the first occurrence of the term can be linked back to Hans Asperger's 1938 lecture, where he made reference to "autistic psychopaths." Hans was unfortunately a Nazi with eugenicist principles, and his outlook on the neurotype helped shape a not so positive narrative that has only begun to be broken in recent years.

When I was a child, I remember being taught about autism from a support worker that would visit my school. Due to my half-brother being diagnosed as autistic before I was born, I already knew quite a lot about it from a very early age. Eventually, the support worker told me I was autistic.

I responded, "Well, yeah. Duh?"

That reaction took her by surprise. I was seven years old at the time, but I already had a deep understanding that I was very different from everyone else I knew. After she dropped what she thought was this big bombshell on me, she told me about Hans Asperger's work. Over the next couple of weeks, she helped me put together a presentation that would teach my class about my condition. The presentation was essentially information about autism, put into bite-sized facts that fellow seven-year-olds could understand, but a lot of that information was based on a Nazi's research, the research of someone who worked to wipe us from existence. This isn't to say all of Hans Asperger's work was completely wrong—and he wasn't the only person to contribute to a misleading idea of what autism is. But as the decades have gone by, we obviously now have a far greater understanding of autism, and, well, we don't listen to Nazis so much anymore.

The first understandings of autism were very rigid, even for years after Hans Nazi era research. The DSM-II (the second edition of the Diagnostic and Statistical Manual of Mental Disorder), published in 1968, described autism as a form of childhood schizophrenia, and it was thought that it came as a result of "cold" parenting, specifically from "unemotional" mothers.

By the time 1980 rolled around, the DSM-III was published, which made clear that schizophrenia and autism were two separate and distinct diagnoses, rooted from biological causes, not environmental. This DSM required that within the first 30 months of life, a patient meet three specific criteria:

- A lack of interest in people,

- Severe impairments in communication,

- And bizarre responses to the environment

The diagnostic criteria were revised in 1987 and were broadened quite greatly. This is when we can see that there was beginning to be some kind of understanding of a spectrum, though we weren't quite there yet. The next DSM, the DSM-IV was then released in 1994 (and revised in 2000), and for the first time officially, the word "spectrum" was used, with "Asperger's Disorder" being the diagnosis for the milder end of that spectrum. In the 2000s, there was a huge rise in people being diagnosed as autistic, but for the most part, only young boys were being diagnosed.

I was born in 2000, and it was clear to my mother that, from a very young age, I was different, and likely autistic. I couldn't talk until I was five and couldn't make friends. School affected me so much that doctors at my local hospital investigated my stomach for months only to decide I was suffering symptoms of extreme stress. I remember being a very literal child—sarcasm was beyond me—and because I couldn't read emotions very well, I always thought everyone was angry at me. The world I grew up in was very alien to me. It was actually my first head teacher that encouraged my parents to strive for an official diagnosis, so that's what they did.

This was a huge struggle, however, doctors were extremely reluctant to diagnose a girl, as autism was still seen as a "boy's disorder," and all the diagnostic criteria was still based on the classic male experience of autism. Luckily though, my parents are stubborn and after a lot of effort,

I became the only girl in my county to be diagnosed in all of 2007. I was officially autistic!

I was a very tech savvy kid, so by the time 2011 rolled around, I was always on the internet. I was very proud of being autistic, and I loved that I experienced the world differently, even if it was difficult sometimes. I never thought that my diagnosis was a problem, I thought the world was at fault for creating a society that didn't welcome and embrace difference. So, I made a Twitter account where I celebrated autism, I got involved in autism advocacy work, and I met other young people like me.

When I started being publicly autistic on the internet, I remember others would praise me for my bravery, I'd be called inspiring for not being afraid to share my diagnosis. I also dealt with a lot of backlash from people who decided I couldn't possibly be autistic because I'm nothing like their autistic relative, or that it was a horrible thing I was passing off my disability as some positive thing.

I've always had a very positive outlook on being autistic though. It's how my brain is wired, it's integral to my very being, take the autism out of me and well… I'm not me anymore. As the years went on, more like-minded autistic people began to share their experiences online and decided to live life unapologetically and freely as autistic people. There were also a lot of people who decided to be public about being autistic whilst sharing how they personally didn't see such a positive side to their neurotype.

I think that's important to be shared too. I've had my days where all I've wanted is to just know what it's like to be "normal" and not have to deal with some of the struggles that come along with being autistic. While these moments are fleeting for me, for others they're not. I think that's exactly what's so important about autistic people using the internet to come together.

It can't be understated just how much the internet has done for autistic people. We've gone from Neurotypical scientists making the rules of what autism is and can be, to hundreds of autistic people now finding each other and exploring who we are together. We make the rules now.

That's not to say there's not still a place for science, but now doctors and scientists can learn from the lived autistic experience. The internet gave us a voice that cannot be silenced, and we're no longer some medical mystery. Girls are now diagnosed at a far higher rate, adults are getting diagnoses that give them answers as to why they've been different their whole lives, and autistic people are becoming more accepted in society.

With the help of the internet, we've been able to educate others about how we really function, and we're breaking down the stereotypes that have confined us since the 1940s. I've watched the public perception about us change so much in such a short time, and it makes me so proud because this is what autistic people have done, we accomplished this for ourselves.

I don't want to put across the image that being autistic is all sunshine and rainbows, even though I celebrate and embrace my differences, it doesn't stop it from being hard occasionally, but that's exactly why it's important that we're celebrated. We're carving out a space for ourselves in society that has never existed before, and, by doing that, we're making our world easier to live in.

I was a very lonely child. I was an outcast that stayed inside playing video games all day because it was so difficult for me to maintain friendships. I'd like to think that if I was growing up today, with the public perception of autism now being so different than what it was 20 years ago, I might have had a little less of that loneliness consuming me. I hope that's how other autistic children now are growing up for the most part, each generation feeling more welcome than the last.

SOURCES:

https://www.autism.org.uk/advice-and-guidance/what-is-autism/the-history-of-autism

https://molecularautism.biomedcentral.com/articles/10.1186/s13229-018-0208-6

https://www.thetransmitter.org/spectrum/leo-kanners-1943-paper-on-autism/

https://www.thetransmitter.org/spectrum/evolution-autism-diagnosis-explained/

The Autism as a Superpower—A Conversation

WE TALKED
WHAT IT MEANS TO BE AUTISTIC
IDENTITY, LIVED EXPERIENCES, STRENGTHS, AND THE FIGHT TO BE UNDERSTOOD

KATHERINE: One thing I like about being autistic is my ability to digest information and fixate on topics that spark my interest, like useless information. Random factoids that don't really help. And go down the rabbit hole.

[…]

COREY: There is no such thing as useless information. It depends on how it's applied.

KATHERINE: I use it for conversation starters.

SCOTT: Thinking about people and not assuming that they are always bad. I've been down so much that sometimes I don't think of people as automatically bad, even though I have to set aside fear as an act of will to engage with people.

JUSTIN H: My ability to improvise humor—I'm not sure everyone else can do that. I can write jokes, and I can find humor in the weirdest places. And probably not the best at making jokes for children, though . . .

COREY: I do as well. How did Vlad the Impaler got their name? It was in a very specific way…

JUSTIN H: He was the king of Romania. Impaling was his favourite form of torture

COREY: He was a king after he was a general, as he fought in wars and s***. So, Vlad the Impaler, he used to impale people with a pike through the butt which would come out through mouth. Then he used to post people up like that after he killed them. I don't know if it's actually true, but from what I understand, he used to be the reason people associate Vlad the Impaler with Dracula. He's the inspiration for Dracula. He used to host parties and put blood in goblets. He used to drink the blood of his victims in the goblets.

JUSTIN H: He did even worse than that. He made prisoners of certain countries eat their comrades as well.

JUSTIN M: I have this thing where it's like I can remember exactly what happened during a certain time, but I can't remember what happened yesterday. So three years ago, I'd have a meeting or something, and I'll know exactly who was sitting where, what they were wearing, what we were talking about. I could say what was in the room and everything. But if you ask me what happened yesterday, I have no clue. I can remember details on where I was and what I was doing for a majority of my life, which is pretty cool.

KATHERINE: You're an actor, right? How does that affect how you do your lines?

JUSTIN M: I only need to look at my lines once or twice, and then I remember them. I kind of just read my script, and then I really don't need to look at it anymore, cuz I already know the lines down pat. I usually look at it once or twice, and then I know it by hand, which is pretty cool.

And in my building, I have this funny trick where I know everybody's buzzer code. Somebody asks me, "What's this person's buzzer number?" And I know exactly what buzzer number it is. All I have to do is just count up from where I am to what their buzzer number is.

I also feel, like, magnets around me. It's really weird. I'll walk up to somebody, and I can sense that there's something there. And I'm like, "You have a magnet on you," and they just look at me stunned. I don't know what it is. I just get all staticy and stuff. It's weird.

Corey: You should open a kiosk at a movie theater with a sign that says, "I can sense magnets - $5."

KATHERINE: There was actually a scientist that implanted a magnet into one of his fingers to be able to sense magnetic fields.

COREY: I wonder if something like that can be passed down genetically over the years.

KATHERINE: I mean, the magnet did work its way out because it's not meant to be in you.

[…]

COREY: If you plant it deep enough inside the body and in a certain part, it'll be harder to get out. So eventually it'll just kind of integrate with your system if you plant it all the way up your arm as opposed to in your finger.

BRIANNA: I don't think I have normal autism. I don't have what a lot of you guys are talking about and that I read about. I definitely didn't get the intelligent part of autism. So, I had the opposite issue.

I struggled with learning in school. But I find that one thing is maybe planning or if I'm into something, I'm extremely into it, maybe beyond what I need to be. So I find that if my mom or somebody needs something done, then they normally come to me because they know it'll get done quickly with detail and stuff. But I definitely wish I had that part.

COREY: Albert Einstein struggled in school and became one of the best minds… It's because of the way school is structured. Not designed for minds with autism.

[…]

BRIANNA: My teacher would sit me in a corner with an iPad, and it wasn't until I was in high school that I learned to self-advocate. That came from being part of community.

ERIC: I have good pattern recognition that helps with playing video games. Like playing Monsters Hunter. I get a sense of how the monsters are going to react and can pick up more quickly than others.

COREY: It's not the type of game I would normally play, but I find that I'm actually getting really good with the physics of games. And the funny thing is all I have to do is throw a grenade once in a game, and now I can practically predict exactly where the trajectory is going to go even before I throw it just by aiming up a certain ways. I've got the physics down within a single throw of a grenade.

ERIC: I think that's another thing with pattern recognition—I knew a lot of things that needed to be done, and could do them quickly, sometimes even tackling projects before they were given to me. Also, I'm very good at writing, because I can just tell when something isn't spelled correctly.

KATHERINE: I tend to find that people assume and I'm lawyering them through an argument. When that's just kind of how my brain works.

COREY: You're trying to prevent it from going into hostile territory.

KATHERINE: If someone commits a logical fallacy, I will point it out, and people really don't like it when you do that. I'm working on how to do that less, as my parents say I'm "lawyering" them and they don't like it. For me, it's almost just being pedantic. I'll say, "you technically didn't say this, or that argument is rhetorical–it isn't based on logic." That is really annoying for people, I've found.

COREY: Yeah, I don't understand why they get upset about that, though. Wouldn't you want to know if you've made a mistake in your argument? Because wouldn't that diffuse the argument or at least help to push the argument along?

KATHERINE: I guess I can see how that would annoy other people. Personally, I think that would be more helpful than anything.

COREY: I've had people describe autism as a super intelligent disability or whatever. It's like some people with autism are way ahead of others…

KATHERINE: I think it really depends on what form of autism you have because people with Aspergers are typically really good at math and that's really helpful. And people assume that if you have Aspergers, you have a higher intelligence than other forms of autism.

[…]

COREY Kearns: I've met a lot of people who categorize autism as if there is a different types, is what I was getting that. But yeah, there are different levels, intensities and so and so forth, right? It's a whole messy branch of different intensities and different types.

ERIC: In high school I had a few issues because I was reserved and I like to think before saying things. So I spoke slowly. When news of my ASD came out, they just started treating me like some kind of moron. They thought I spoke slowly because I didn't understand them.

DEBBIE: There's a common assumption that someone who is autistic is antisocial. That they walk around thinking, and the reason they don't make eye contact is that they're not interested in having or forming relationships, friendships, and so on. Elliot is the complete opposite. He's an extrovert who loves social environments and meeting new people. So I find that misperception is still very much out there. And the other one I still hear to date is that autism is only found in males. And I still hear that today. We had quite a few friends they missed, who did not have a diagnosis until later in life because back then professionals just didn't acknowledge autism in girls. I think we've come a little bit of a ways, but I still hear it from the general population.

CIARA: I wrote about it my section—I knew I had autism but they didn't test me until later than they did my brother just because I'm female.

KATHERINE: I'm far more inclined to want to make friends with other autistic people because I communicate better with them. So, maybe what people perceive as autistics being antisocial is that socializing with neurotypical people is harder. It's just easier to be friends with someone else with autism because we're more likely to be on the same wavelength.

[…]

~*~

AKOSUA: It's called a disorder. It's called a disability. Is that something that bothers you? Or do you think that's right? Does that impact you or is it a trigger at all, as it suggests there is something that needs to be fixed?

COREY: I'd call a disability. Call it whatever it is at the end of the day. A word is a word. It doesn't really need to have an impact if I don't want it to.

KATHERINE: I can understand why words like disability disorder would be seen as insensitive because obviously it implies that there's something wrong with us. But like Corey said, personally, it doesn't really bother me. It's just something where you are used to hearing it, but maybe that is something that needs to be rectified. Maybe we don't need to be used to hearing about how disordered we are, because personally, I consider it to be an improvement.

COREY: Agreed. It's easier to be direct and straightforward, which is far less confusing. A lot more productive.

KATHERINE: Exactly. I love being autistic.

[...]

AKOSUA: Being too focused on the stuff on the internet can make lots of people hate themselves.

KATHERINE: I think a lot of that sort of self-hatred and self-loathing about being autistic is typically based off of the people that we surround ourselves with. Because if you're around people who understand you and understand your needs, there's no real reason for you to hate being autistic. If you're not in an environment where you're constantly being overstimulated or we can't communicate with people, it's kind of just a neutral state of being. It's just like I'm just autistic. This is just how I am. I think for a lot of people, autism within isn't the issue. It's the neurotypical world outside.

[...]

CIARA: I have multiple other disabilities. So in my perspective, autism is the least disabling of them, and it doesn't bother me to be called disabled. By definition. It is still a disability, but it's very individualized. I think that society being built for cis-neurotypicals is more disabling than autism itself honestly.

OWEN: I was put in a special class for autistic students in high school and I hated having to walk in the room. We had this assignment that was supposed to be career research based on what you want to do for a living. I said I wanted to be an entrepreneur. So the teacher says, "You can't be an entrepreneur because you're autistic."

[ALL - murmurs and "wow"]

OWEN: So, at the time, everyone was talking about this cruise ship that drove into an island. It was in the news every day. It was on my mind, so I said, "Fine. I want to be a cruise ship driver."
I knew, realistically, even though it would be a cool job, I wasn't going to do that. It's just that I didn't give a s*** if she tried to talk me out of being a cruise ship driver because I didn't want to do that.

COREY: That's awesome. Yeah. It's like, "Okay, I'm gonna do this just because I want to and if you try to tell me differently, well screw you." I like that. That's awesome. That's the same mentality as me.

KATHERINE: Yeah, I can relate to that!

OWEN: It seemed like all they wanted to do in that class was back you into accepting your life would be garbage. So, it felt good saying this. And she did try to talk me out of researching that career.

Then we had to do this exercise, which was like Poverty 101. It was like how to live in poverty. You were supposed to look up how much things cost and create a budget for once you left school. And I was looking up the costs for a car, and they didn't like that. They kept giving me s***, saying, "There's no way you are going to be able to afford a car. Blah blah blah. Aren't you learning anything from this class?" And before I left that school, I showed up with a car, my own car that I bought. It was only a couple months before the end of school, but still!

KATHERINE: I can't imagine communicating to someone that you can't do something because you're autistic.

AKOSUA: I can understand now why you hated that class.

[...]

KATHERINE: I don't know if this is universal or not, but I found that when I was in the special ed class, a lot of it was focused on how to not be autistic rather than how to learn as someone with autism.

COREY: It was almost like they're trying to rehabilitate you.

KATHERINE: That's how it felt. They had these signs up that would show you how not to act. It was behavioral therapy almost. They had this five-point system, and, on the system, there was a smiley face as Level One and just progressively worsening sad and upset faced emojis to Level Five. This is for autistic people to show their stress level in a scenario, so, if they were feeling, say, Level Five, the educator would be able to understand that.

My school used the system as a tool of invalidation against autistic people. So, they would say to me if I was having a Level Five reaction, "You are having a Level Five reaction to a Level One scenario."

COREY Kearns: I've had similar experiences to that. Aside from being autistic, I was diagnosed with schizoaffective disorder bipolar type at age eight.

I was with a group home agency, and they had a psychiatrist on the payroll, so everybody went to see her. Instead of focusing on all the other symptoms I was dealing with–like hallucinations, muscle spasms, cramps, and reactions to the medication and what-not–she fixated on the rocking back and forth. She was fixated on where my hands were when I was sitting and talking with her. Her fixations were about making me not stand out, as opposed to the actual problems that were there. About 90 percent of our conversation was about this. It would be "Corey, your hands are and your hands aren't in your lap–they should be folded nicely. Corey, you're rocking back and forth. Corey, you're not looking directly into my eyes."

What the hell? Yeah, exactly.

CIARA: Yeah, I see that.

WAYMAN: I find it strange that no one has mentioned difficulty with exams. I had no workable school support systems, but exams were my biggest problem. Exams always triggered high levels of tension that so clouded my ability to think/reason that I could not even understand most of the questions. I have memories of sitting exams where I'd spent most of the allocated time trying to find even one question that made enough sense that I could even attempt an answer.

KATHERINE: I know that my other autistic brethren have experienced this.

[...]

~*~

AKOSUA: We all need communities where we can feel safer, seen, celebrated, and supported. And that's what we get from these conversations. And I hope that is what this book will do for people.

"YOUR VOICE MATTERS"

Every perspective enriches the conversation. As you reflect on the ideas shared here, we encourage you to keep the dialogue alive—whether it's with your friends, family, or community. Share your thoughts, your questions, and your experiences. Together, we can create more understanding and inclusion.

Earth-Bound Explorer
By Justin Milner

I was diagnosed with Asperger Syndrome (autism) when I was about five years old.

When I was a kid, I wanted to be an astronaut. That was a dream of mine; to explore other planets and the universe to see what is beyond Earth. I was often treated unfairly by my peers and teachers, and other adults told me that my dream was too stupid and far from reality. You need a lot of money, years of education, and, because of my disability, it was not possible. So, I kept my dreams silent from everyone after that.

In my early 20s I had a new objective, a goal that I wanted to travel to explore all the amazing places Canada has to offer. I used social media to showcase everything that I'm up to in life. Today I am in my 30s and living my dream. I take great pleasure when people say to me "I love your pictures" and "You always find the greatest places to go." I am living my dream every day, and I love every moment of it.

"An Underachiever" Who Doesn't Relate Well to Others
By Wayman Edward Sole

I am called wes (always in lowercase), based on my initials. Shortly after birth, I required corrective surgery to repair a life-threatening digestive tract defect. I am dyslexic. To my knowledge, I have never been formally diagnosed as autistic, but I do consider myself to be living on the spectrum.

I am 87 years old and live in London, Ontario, Canada. From birth, I was equipped with a world view that differed significantly from the accepted norm. I did not relate well to others or with my environment, and early school was more akin to a place of fear and confusion than a place for fun and learning. And yes, it was also a place to do battle with teachers.

But, doing battle didn't help, so I gradually developed a set of survival skills—some may say coping skills—that allowed me to figuratively disappear in a classroom. My thought was, if I don't say or do anything to attract attention, then perhaps nobody would pay any attention to me. This worked remarkably well except that, in doing so, I separated myself from much needed help. Whatever the reason, I was a poor scholastic achiever and many of my public-school report cards carried the phrases "not performing up to potential," "an underachiever," or similar comments.

At home my parents taught us acceptable social skills and self-discipline from a very early age. In my case, this process was, at times, a battle of wills. Fortunately, my parents accepted this and continued to encourage me to put forth my best effort.

Looking back, I now realize my parents always made sure I was challenged to succeed within whatever bounds seemed to exist. For example, mechanical building bits, and a number of clocks and watches to disassemble and reassemble, mostly mechanical things. Always a challenge, and I developed very good eye-hand dexterity that I still enjoy. Then and until very recently, I did not realize my learning struggles were any different from those experienced by anyone else. Consequently, I didn't think that I was different so far as learning is concerned.

I was in the Royal Canadian Air Force for eight years and was initially posted to Moose Jaw, Saskatchewan, and then to France, where I was Honourably Released. For most of my life, I worked in various positions in Technical Computing. I am a widower and have two daughters. I also worked helping dyslexic children thrive and found a way to get through to nonverbal, non-social kids on the spectrum, using clay and modelling as a medium for doing that.

Not My Real Name
By Owen Bryan

was told I had autism when I was 13. My mother believed it and made a career out of it. Honestly. But I have fought against the diagnosis as I just didn't have anything in common with the people in the special ed classes they put me in. I think I've just been so sad because my real dad died when I was two years old. I think my problem is trauma, but all teachers and my mom and adults wanted me to do was deal with autism. Like, the other guys in the class were unable to talk, and I was nothing like them. It was so stupid to have me in those classes, unhelpful. How was it possible that I was more like them in the room than like the people walking past it?

And, so you know, this isn't my real name. I want to tell my story, but I don't want any comments on it. I don't want people to know what a loser I am as then I'll never have a chance at "a life." I'm online a lot, and I see comments about what people think of people like me all the time. Then, when I say things like this to my mom, she'll say, "Did you know Albert Einstein was on the spectrum? And the guy who created Pokémon? Steve Jobs, too." Big deal. I'm here, broke and unable to get a job. They were (or are) all rich. It is easier to be anything if you are rich.

Did you know that, like, 80 percent of autistic people are unemployed? That's what I say to my mom when she tells me all that shit. I want a good job. I want to make a lot of money. I want a nice house all to myself—I could practically build one on my own.

I once worked as a carpenter, but it ended badly. Almost drove me nuts. They wanted me to do overtime, and I could hardly make it through a day. No way was I going to work even a single extra hour to take that guy's abuse. My boss was such an asshole! But there were some good things about having that job: the dollars. That's all. I just could not cope with the mean people and how they'd get on my case because I'm shy and because I wouldn't work overtime.

It made me so mad being there. I'd get so mad because everyone used to just yell at me (and yeah: they yelled at each other too—that's how they spoke). But I couldn't deal with it. It made me madder that I couldn't do anything about it. Why couldn't I do anything about it? Because I'm shy. I hate shyness more than autism.

I want a better life, but I'm tired of trying. It feels like since I left high school, I've been trying and have gotten nowhere. We moved away from the country, which I loved. I used to love to cut the lawn on the tractor. I used to love fixing that tractor as it was always breaking down. We had to move because my mom split up with my step-dad and there were no jobs where we used to live. Now we live in a city in an apartment—with no grass to cut and no snow to shovel. I can't even go outside to fix my car as we don't have a driveway. My brother has his own troubles (although at least he has friends online and in real life) and my sisters are away at university.

They are all younger than me.

I tried to go to university, but I couldn't deal with all the f***ing group projects. Every time I'd go in a room, the professor would say "find a partner" or something like that. By the end of the first term, I was going nuts. I felt my head would explode when I thought about it at home, when I was on the way there, when I was on the way home from there, and most of all, when I was actually there. I'd sit there, and I'd be so mad and sad that all I could do was try not to lose my mind in class—it was that bad. And people were looking at me—they had these big windows by some classrooms. I know some girls were looking at me even from outside of the class and I saw someone laughing and looking at me.

So, I quit.

I had to pay back a lot of money, but I did pay it back. That was when I was 19. It's ten years later–I'll be 30 in a few days. Now I'm taking a course online, and I'm almost finished. I've pushed hard to do it, and my marks are always in the nineties. I hope I can get work when I'm done, as I've tried working for other people, and it never works out. So, I'm going to work for myself. Mom will get the clients; she can deal with them, and I'll do the work.

That's our plan.

I Was Lost, Then Found Humanity Inside a Hospital
By Robert Williams

My name is Robert, and I'm in my forties. When I was in my late teens, a long time ago now, I was diagnosed with autism. At the time, I was looking for ways in which to rebel in society because I was left wondering why I felt so separate from everyone else. The doctors, teachers, and my family were looking to understand why I acted as I did.

When I look back after all these years, I think that everything has been a lesson rather than a curse that has been laid upon me. But back then, I continued on a path which led me to being admitted into a hospital for the first time. In the hospital, I met people who became my friends. They were to me more human than anyone else on the outside.

Within the hospital, they helped. I was in this place with these new friends, and, for the first time, I could relate to people. These people cared, even though, like me, many were there because they had done things that they regretted. I saw the greatness in them. I remember them to this day as good people. That changed things for me.

Dreaming with All Senses on High
By Scott R. Dawson

My name is Scott Robert Dawson, and I live in Belleville, Ontario. I'm in my 60s.

For pretty much all of my life, I've known that I was "different." Always, I've struggled with social communication. I had no knowledge of autism though; if I had heard of it at all, I had the impression of someone cowering away from the world, unable to communicate. In public and high school, I thought that I just needed to find the right social key, the right combination of hairstyle or clothing perhaps, and then I would suddenly be popular and liked.

Only during years of counselling would I learn how deep my differences went. As an example, I learned that many (most?) people can instantly recognize the identity of someone in their face. I have always had to guess who people are from clues like hairstyle, height, build, gait, clothing, etc. This kind of thing is so basic that it never occurs to most people that others could have a different experience. My counselor and I worked backwards looking at my experiences, and yes, definitely, it would have affected how people related to me.

And, I have always had full-colour dreams with sound, touch, even smell. Sometimes, I remember them and write them down or draw them. I often get stories this way. (Yes, I even make stories in my sleep). I was very surprised to meet someone whose dreams were just words, no pictures at all.

And autism? I stumbled on that by accident. I started reading Temple Grandin's *Thinking in Pictures*, and I began to wonder, why do her experiences sound so familiar? But she's 'on the spectrum', and yes, my counselors said that it was likely that I am too.

So here I am…

I Showed Them!
By Brianna Longhenry

Hi, I'm Brianna. I'm 22, and I'm a mom. I have a two-year-old. Besides caring for my son, my favourite things is going to my cottage and going for ATV rides. Things are better, as my whole childhood and most of my teenage years I always thought there was something wrong with me. Mostly with education and social environments. I remember always feeling trapped within my skin. Now at the age of 22, I no longer feel trapped—I just feel not understood, if that even makes sense.

In grade six, I had a diagnosis of Asperger's syndrome, or high functioning autism. At that time, I was displaying typical signs: repetitive behaviour, sensitivity to visual/audio stimuli, and difficulties in understanding body language and really understanding any kind of learning. As a toddler, I would learn my colours and really be obsessed with repeating my colors, then my daycare would focus on counting, and, by the next week, I could count to 100—but no longer knew my colours. I still struggle with similar learning issues. I become so hyper focused on something and almost forget the previous thing I was focused on. I have to retrain my brain constantly.

During middle school, I remember my teachers sending me to the back of the classroom to play on my iPad. I'd sit back there and just feel so separated from the rest of the class, and I'd spend hours playing Minecraft on the iPad, wishing I would be asked to participate in any class discussions or even work. I remember a few occasions in grade seven, how teachers made me feel like I was worthless.

One time, I handed in a class project that the class was working on. I took the project home and worked hard on it for days and was excited to hand something in for the first time. A few hours after I handed in my project, I witnessed my teacher put it through the paper shredder and then hand everyone else back their projects with their grade marked in the corner. I remember wanting to scream out and ask what my grade was, but then thinking my project must have been so horrible that is why he shredded it.

Another time, we had a substitute teacher. I used to get excited when we got substitute teachers as they didn't know me, so I would be treated like the rest of the class. I even got to participate the same as the others. On this occasion, I didn't understand the instructions for the assignment. I bravely walked to the front of the classroom and explained that I had autism and if she could help by explaining the assignment in different way, an easier way for me to understand. The teacher started speaking very loud but slow, like I had a hearing problem. I stopped her and said "I'm not deaf, you don't need to speak to me like that. If you could just explain it differently."

In grade eight, my family doctor basically told my parents not to send me to high school and to instead work on teaching me basic life skills. The doctor said that with my education level, I would not succeed in life and basically told my parents how I could get financial help (welfare or disability). I remember driving home that day in the back seat of the car and saying to my mom, "Am I really a failure? Is he right that I won't go anywhere in life?"

My Mom, my biggest supporter, laughed and said, "Brianna, together we are going to show them how wrong they are, you can do absolutely anything you want in life." That day, I started teaching myself. I'd go onto Google and join home school class groups, self-taught reading and math. I was determined not to be labeled as unfixable.

I did graduate high school with an IEP and lots of work, and I remember, a week after getting my diploma, sending a quick email to that doctor who straight out told my parents not to waste years on high school but to just teach me life skills. If I can give any advice to anyone with autism… DO NOT allow others to put you down or put you in categories like that. You can do anything you want to—it might just take longer than it does for others without a disability.

I Am
By Corey Kearns

I grew up all over the place.
I am a free-spirited person
I value choice, expression, and authenticity
Above most other things.
I have a wide range of humour
And a knack for story telling
As well as a fairly wide range of artistic talents.
I am always my unapologetic self
No matter the situation
And I refuse to be anything but.
I struggle with expressing myself sometimes
But that doesn't stop me from finding a way to try.
I live with a fair amount of health problems that make it hard to live life
But I would rather pay the cost of enjoying myself
Than not enjoy myself at all.
I enjoy seeing how people choose to use their freedom
To act how they see fit in situations
Because it teaches you a lot
About them as a person.
At the end of the day,
I am a joker, a mediator, a storyteller, a gamer, and a fighter.
I am resilient, passionate, free, and compassionate.
Regardless of whatever side I show,
You can count on the fact that it will always
Be completely and unequivocally me
Right down the loose-fitting clothes
And laid-back approach
I take to
Everything.

Bloodshade94
Corey Kearns

My name is Corey James Shawn Kearns, and I was born in the Oshawa General Hospital in Oshawa, Ontario, Canada. I grew up in group homes from the age of six to 19. I have a dog named Ozzie and a cat named Olaf.

I am a passionate gamer, story writer, and artist who enjoys a wide variety of genres. I love playing Dungeons and Dragons, reading, and exploring new things in life. I excel at character design, dark and intense story writing, as well as strategy. I love technology, and I find sounds involving water to be very calming.

I was born with a club foot, underdeveloped retinas, and have wide, wide range of mental health diagnoses. I was diagnosed with autism and Schizoid-Affective Disorder: Bipolar Type around the age of eight. I was diagnosed with C-PTSD around the age of 27-28 while I was an outpatient at Ontario Shores Centre for Mental Health in Whitby, Ontario.

I struggle with depression, connecting, and sometimes motivation and focus. I struggle with a lot of intense PTSD moments from a wide range of sources. I'm so desensitized from all the trauma I've lived through that if it wasn't for the fact I have shared some of my story and people have confirmed I have been through a lot, I would still be shrugging it off trying to convince myself I have no right to be traumatized.

I got really into online gaming when I was around, twenty and my online friends gave me the nickname "Shade" because my Gamertag is BloodShade94. It is my favorite nickname and honestly my preferred alias. I am very fond of using aliases in place of my real name whenever possible.

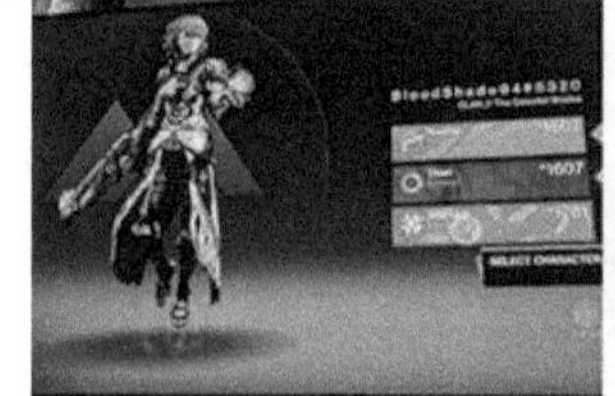 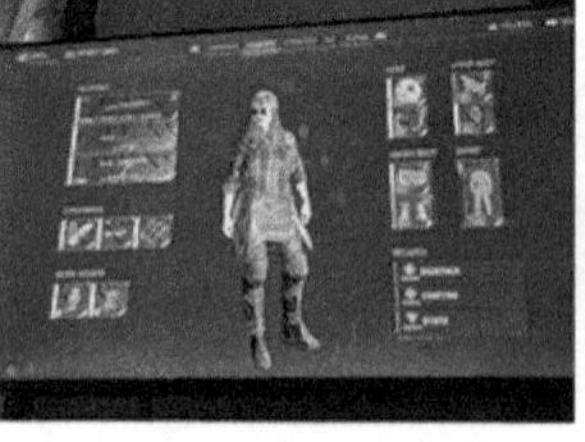 

I Am
By Justin Humphreys

I am a person who loves spicy food
And smell of spicy sausage soup—
It smells so wonderful.
I hear dogs bark when the wind blows.
Play some Black Sabbath
Preferably their song "Paranoid."
It's a song that makes me happy—
and it can help me not hear my mom's music,
In effect, it keeps my ears from bleeding and me going deaf.
I am funny!
I prefer to have people around to
Socialize with.
I love being around family and friends
And hate to be alone.
Playing video games, guitar, and pickle ball are lots of fun.
Looking forward to Summer Peloza*.

*A series of events managed by charity, Autism Home Base in Durham Region, Ontario, Canada.

Self-Acceptance as an Autistic Adult
By Katherine Layne

I saw myself as half-witted and less than the other students. Meeting other autistic people helped me to understand myself and for me acceptance comes from finding solidarity with other autistic people.

My Diagnosis:

- When I was six my dad noticed physical and social traits which included discomfort with eye contact, mannerisms, failure to respond to social cues.

- He began to research traits of neurodivergent individuals

- At first, he was nervous about describing the differences he noticed and his research to my biological mother, fearing she would be insulted

- During this period of my life, I was experiencing behavioural issues, anger, defiance etc.,

- A family friend who was a social worker with the government's Children's Aid Society suggested that I may have had some sort of disorder, noticing traits of ADHD and autism

- When my stepdad first met me, he looked into my behavior as he thought it could be related to autism

- Around the time my stepdad had made his concerns known, my Grade 1 teacher also stated that she believed that I had some sort of disability.

My Perception of Myself

How I came to perceive myself as someone with autism was fundamentally based on the perceptions of the authority figures around me. Because the people in power didn't understand autism, I didn't understand autism. As a child, it was assumed I didn't listen, although I did listen—I lacked the ability to remember what the people were saying. The authority figures believed that being autistic meant a student needed to be fixed, that they were deficient, so naturally I didn't want to be deficient. I used to lament to my parents how badly I just wanted to be "normal."

So, for years, I ignored my autism, tried the best I could to not act autistic. I masked who I was, and I pretended so hard to be something I wasn't that I eventually believed I wasn't autistic. I believed that there must've been some sort of mistake, it was simply a result of helicopter parents trying to shelter me. I began to refuse help, any sort of aid I was provided (such as fidget toys or a rocking chair). I would deny these supports out of fear that I would be mocked relentlessly by my peers. Because I had the ability to refuse these aids, because I could function without them, I assumed I wasn't autistic, a lie I fed myself for years.

I was unhappy, but I didn't know why. I was empty, but I couldn't understand what that void meant. I was an innocuous shell. For years I remained this way, not understanding why I couldn't communicate with my peers, and why others perceived me as different. I felt broken, like a computer unable to process code. I was defective, and yet my defect was invisible to everyone besides myself.

I felt this way for years until I met others like me. It took a while because I would've never willingly associated with someone who was openly autistic. At the time, I believed they were all "retards," as my peers would say. And if I was to keep this defect a secret, I could not associate with defective people. I had to be a sleeper agent, an autistic spy in neurotypical garb. I felt like I was in espionage, infiltrating my own life; if I were near "retards," it would only be a matter of time before one of those autistic James Bonds found me. I've always felt a pull to other autistic people, like we exist on the same wavelength. I knew who to avoid.

I understood them in ways I never really understood others. It was like we spoke the same language, but not a language you can write. It was a feeling, something you couldn't taste, smell or touch, but something born within our minds that made us different from anyone else. It was a kinship between an autistically closeted found family. The draw was strong. I had found my people, and I didn't know why.

I also didn't know what made them "mine." It wasn't our interests or lifestyle choices or anything like that, it was the solidarity of finding someone you knew in a sea of strangers. It was like falling down flights of stairs, with each impact there was the painful realization that I wasn't the only person like me, that I wouldn't eventually change and grow out of it. Gravity unwillingly pulled me towards this conclusion. I felt it as it happened maybe not consciously, but I felt it. I could tell I was getting closer to the answer. I felt I was finding myself, getting closer to knowing who I was, closer to the bottom of the steps. I couldn't simply ignore who I was because I saw myself reflected at me, staring into my eyes.

I didn't have the words to say this at the time, but that's how it felt. When you're made to be "the other" your entire life, it hurts you like getting hit by a truck when you find someone else like you, and it doesn't matter if they have different interests or different everything; they're still like you on a fundamental level.

Despite describing this feeling in detail now, at the time, I still lacked an understanding and avoided the one word that should be there as the thing that connected us—autism.

I only ever understood what autism was through these othered people. They weren't initially open about having autism; in fact, a lot of them were in a similar state of denial as myself. But, like me, as they started to accept themselves and used the language I use today, the word autism was no longer a dirty word. It was made clean by their usage.

My friends understood themselves as autistic, and when they expressed this, it only took a quick assessment on my part to notice. I was way more like these "retards" than I was like any neurotypical person I had ever met. And that was my turning point into self-acceptance.

It was simple groupthink behavior. They wore headphones when noise was loud, so I tried it and realized that it wasn't normal to feel like you're going to explode while doing the dishes. And, eventually, I began to use the language they used—like overstimulation, fidgeting/stimming.

To my parents, it must have seemed as though I had somehow become "more autistic." It was difficult for them to accept at first. But what I came to realize was it was the crumbling of a mask eight years in the making—an act that I had kept up for most of my life at that point. Something so difficult to break down but so relieving. It was terrifying showing bare skin like that, but it was necessary for me to heal.

And with every bandage, every layer of the mask, I took off, I became more fearful of what lay beneath, what internal secret I had kept from myself and the world. Maybe I would uncover something bad? Maybe no one would accept me? But I kept peeling the bandages off and letting the sun burn my skin. I had to explain to people around me that I was always like this, but they never saw it. *I* never saw it.

In the process of unmasking, of removing the crutch I had been relying on, I was forced to learn how to live without it, how to take care of myself as someone with autism. I finally had something to explain why it was I didn't understand things, why I couldn't complete tasks.

I paid attention to myself more than I ever had in my life. Now when I became overstimulated, I felt it, and I could logically discern when it would happen. I felt tense and my brain hurt whenever I did the dishes, or when a car engine would rev, or when at a loud event. So going off of these premises, starting to accept what was real about me, if I knew I would be around such places, it would logically follow that the loud noises would hurt me, so then I wore headphones. I didn't have to pretend I wasn't in pain. I didn't have to mask my pain as I could wear headphones and prevent it. I found that I felt uncomfortable sitting still, something I tried in vain to train myself to do, so I tried not to do that. Whenever I needed to move, I just moved.

I felt better.

The primary lesson was to do what makes you comfortable. When I needed to leave a situation, I would, because when I did, I would feel comfortable. I gave into my urges. I would make noises when I felt like it. I would shake my leg when sitting still. And I would put on headphones when I needed to. I felt better—like I could finally act human again.

I learned to accept myself as autistic by giving myself what I needed. I stopped worrying and trying to guess what a "normal" person would do. I just worried about myself. Whether I was autistic or not didn't matter. I stopped worrying about what other people thought of me, because I now know that the only people that really matter are the ones that accept me as I really am.

Part 2:
Strengths: What We Love to Do!

Independence, Travelling, & Acting
By Justin Milner

Hi, I'm Justin Milner. I'm a 30-something year old man born November 11, 1991. I live in Oshawa Ontario, Canada. I was bullied and harassed because of my disability, even going into adulthood. But I always do the things I love, and this helps me stay positive.

I enjoy nature, photography, painting, theater, camping, music, movies, cars, the 80s, acting, and the great outdoors. Since COVID-19, I have had a new ambition in life to visit every Provincial Park in Ontario. I have explored 88 out of 308. Some of the places I've been to are Algonquin, Balsam Lake, Bass Lake, Bon Echo, Bronte Creek, Charleston Lake, Darlington, Earl Rowe, Emily, Ferries, Killbear, Long Point, Mara, McRea Point, Mono Cliffs, Petroglyphs, Presqu'ile, Rock Point, Sandbanks, Selkirk, Sibbald Point, Silent Lake, Wasaga Beach just to name a few. My long-term goal is to live in an RV and travel across Canada.

Since the COVID-19 pandemic is over, it feels like my life is getting back on track. I'm back to working on community theatre production not just at Oshawa Little Theatre but at other community theatres as well. At work (Sobeys), it has been getting a lot better over the years; it is less stressful now. I have a small group of friends now, which is nice, and my relationship with my family is a work in progress. What gives me the strength to keep going is when people notice the things that I do every day and compliment me on it. Just makes my day. I feel so good to hear that they are taking an interest in my life. At the end of it all, I know I am living my best. As for my future, I don not know what is going to happen. I am just happy for the ride and grateful for everything that has happened.

I went to Eastgate High School, and in Grade 11, did co-op at Sobeys grocery store. They liked me so much that I got hired right after my co-op was finished at 16 years old; years later, I'm still at the same job.

After high school, I was able to attend a program at Durham College called Community Integration through Co-operative Education. It's a two-year program designed to give individuals with intellectual disabilities or challenges the opportunity to go to college and experience it first hand. Through my program at college, I had a few co-ops at Durham Radio, Durham Shoestring Performers, and Oshawa Little Theatre. I fell in love with OLT and theatre instantly and never left. I volunteer my free time at Oshawa Little Theatre and am working my way through the organization, I even became Vice President for a few years.

I've worked in over 40 different productions as a producer, stage manager, and in lighting, sound, set, props, and costumes. I've worked backstage and onstage—pretty much everywhere. I've worked on shows like *Footloose, West Side Story, Music 36, Master Class, Anne of Green Gables, Beauty and the Beast, The Sound of Music, Elf, Into the Woods, Barefoot in the Park,* and *Guys and Dolls,* to name a few.

I have been trying to prove myself at Oshawa Little Theatre over the years. Being part of something wonderful made me work very hard and it worked! I get asked all the time to be involved in different areas of the theatre and people are glad to have me on the team. As of today, I am the Bar Manager and loving every moment of it.

I like to think of myself as an adventurer, exploring new places and trying new things. For the most part adventure is being in the great outdoors. I have the same routine every week and sometimes every day. My life schedule is so organized and routine, I can make an art out of it; I even have random trips and activities planned.

Bronte Creek

Black Creek Pioneer Village

Oshawa Little Theatre at Durham Pride 2023

Canoe Lake

Nipissing, Ontario

Oshawa Generals

Ganaraska Treetop Trekking

Master Class Oshawa Little Theatre

Sceaming Heads

Rouge National Urban Park

Killbear Sunset Rocks "The Tree"

Stoick Axe Throwing

Me in the production of *Elf, The Musical*, Oshawa Little Theatre 2023

Kingston Penitentiary

Sandbanks Provincial Park

The Bay of Quinte, an overview from Lake on the Mountain, from a Road Trip to Prince Edward County in October, 2021.

Bon Echo, a view from my campsite of the Upper Mazinaw Lake in the morning, May, 2019.

Camp 30 in Bowmanville, Ontario. I found a very interesting place to explore with a bit of history as a POV Camp.

Cobourg Beach was one of my favorite beaches to go to every couple of weeks, and I spend hours relaxing in the sun.

Sunrise at Darlington Provincial Park. I enjoy sitting at the deck at McLaughlin Bay, watching the sun go up and down after a long day.

Mono Cliffs Provincial Park, walking though the amazing cliffs in Shelburne, Ontario in 2021

Denise Crosby Fan Expo

Fan Expo 2019, Toronto, meeting Denise Crosby in person and having a coffee at the Central Perk Cafe from Friends.

Justin holding a tarantula for the first time, cornering my fear of spiders and bugs.

Wildlife at McRea Point, it's one of the smallest camping grounds in Ontario with tons of great views and lots of wildlife.

At the Rosebud Motel from Schitt's Creek, it's pretty cool visiting a place that you only see on television.

Sandbanks Provincial Park is one of my favourite parks, it feels like you're down south without actually going south. It was also the filming place of one of my favourite: songs "Honeymoon Suite Wave Babies."

Oshawa Little Theatre the cast and crew of Footloose 2019 my 30th production at OLT on the costume and set team.

A view of Niagara Falls from the Sky Tower 2020

Camping at Killbear Provincial Park along the Georgian Bay in June 2022.

One of my favorite productions at Oshawa Little Theatre and my 35th Show: *The Sound of Music* November, 2022.

Excelling & Uplifting All Abilities Sports
By Elliot Smith

Autism has helped me get opportunities, because it has opened doors to possibilities. I could never play on a sports team when I was younger, because no one understood my disability, and they could not make accommodations. Later in life, I tried a new way of sport called Mixed Ability Sport where players with and without disabilities play and everyone was included. Everyone is treated the same, and everyone is welcome based on age, gender, cultural/religious background, and/or disability. I joined a Mixed Ability team with the Oshawa Vikings Rugby League and am now the co-captain for that team.

I have played in tournaments overseas. Our team came in second out of 24 other countries at the International Mixed Ability Tournament (IMART) in June of 2022. I was also selected as one of five Canadians to play in Belfast with the MARIs (Mixed Ability Rugby Invitational), where players were selected to play as one team from all over the world. We are now training for our next IMART in Pamplona, Spain in June of 2025.

I have written two children's books, called *Mateo's Mixed Ability Match* and *Elliot's Excellent MARIs Match,* about my experiences playing sports. I also had a documentary made about my rugby life called *Advantage Gained,* produced by Rob Viscarids. These opportunities helped me get an invitation to sit on the Board of Directors at the Oshawa Vikings Rugby Club. I applied for an Autism Speak Grant and was able to use the money to build the first sensory room at the club, so athletes have a place to go if they feel overwhelmed.

My autism has also helped me be an advocate on many committees in the community, including the Sport and Inclusion team at the Abilities Centre, the Youth Advisory Committee at Grandview, and the Youth Advisory Committee at Jays Care. My committee work and my sport experience both helped me get a job at the Abilities Centre, where I now work a few days a week as a Physical Fitness and Literacy Associate, as well as a Mixed Ability Sport Facilitator.

My autism and ADHD mean I am very active and have to keep myself busy, so I also play a lot of other sports too, such as Mixed Ability Archery, All Abilities Soccer, and Special Olympics Softball, as well as Challenger Baseball.

It was not always easy though to get to where I am. Because of my autism, I faced a lot of barriers. Too often, I was treated differently because no one understood my disability and did not know how to make accommodations for me. When I was in my teenage years, kids were not very nice, and I got bullied at high school. As I got older, I met a bunch of new friends that were far more mature than kids in my later years of elementary school and even going into high school.

Kids accepted me outside of school because they knew right away why I was being mistreated. I found out about these amazing friends, and they even faced barriers as well, and they accepted me as friends ever since. They were nice, happy, and wanted to have me as their friend too. I have had to learn how to advocate for myself, even at my work, so I can make sure I am getting accommodations that will help me be the best I can be.

Pets and Passions
By Corey Kearns

I got Ozzie when I was about 21 years old, and he has changed my life a lot. I got him from a friend of my mum, who got him from an older couple, and they got him from this father and son who abandoned him in the old couple's basement. Ozzie is a very social dog with a persistent personality, he loves giving baths, and he's great with kids, as well as little dogs. Ozzie isn't picky at all. In fact, I had to take him to the vet one time and was warned that getting dogs to take pills is difficult. He said I'd have to hide the medication in his food or trick him to take them. But not Ozzie. He ate the medication straight from my hands like they were treats. Ozzie is a fairly old dog right now, but he still has lots of puppy energy.

I got Olaf from my cousin because their older cat was losing their fur from Olaf's antics, or, at least, that's my understanding. Olaf is a very chill cat. You can hold him upside down, and he just chills there. You can hold him like a baby, and he will just lay there content. My cousin taught him to grip things that you bring close to him with his paws when you hold him like a baby too. Olaf is a very affectionate kitty, but he can also be a real jerk. Sometimes he will scratch a wall or the couch and stare at you while doing it. If you chase him out of the room, he will stop when you stop and then follow you back to resume what he was doing. He isn't scared of spray bottles, and he loves his cat nip.

Olaf and Ozzie are very much like brothers, they eat each other's food, are jealous of the attention the other gets, and they fight over toys. Both my pets have played a huge part in helping me climb out of the shell I grew up in. They have made a huge difference in helping me reconnect with my emotions after the group homes too. I love my pets. They are my best friends and make my home feel full.

I am passionate about a few stories and some of the mediums used to tell them, like art, games, and books. I discovered my passion for art when I was in school. At first, it was a way for me to cope and work through my trauma. Then I took art classes in high school, and my art teacher was impressed with my capabilities. She kept recommending her more challenging classes to me each year, and I was happy to take them. I did clay work, sketching, and shading, watercolour painting, and even stencil art with paint, water pressure guns, and t-shirts. I went to Trillium College for game design, where I learned about 3D modelling and 2D modelling. I also learned about coding and level building as well. I went to Durham College about a year after, where I learned about sculpting details into 3D models and designing textures, as well as materials for 3D models.

I've been playing video games since I was four, but I didn't discover my passion for them until high school. I became an avid gamer when I moved home, and gaming started out as a means of coping with the isolation and trauma I had been forced to endure in the system. I played on a variety of different platforms and owned a few different ones too. I played online games to work through my social anxiety, and I developed an impressive gaming library while I was at it. I discovered that I enjoyed a wide genre of games and became very interested in the inner workings of the game mechanics.

I took creative writing in high school, but I didn't discover my passion for story writing until I was asked to host some Dungeons and Dragons sessions for the Autism Home Bases summer palooza event. I made up my own story, created my own character sheets and rules, then, from there, I spun an elaborate and eventful story that got a lot of praise from the members. I joined a group called creative expression through the Autism Home Base as a recommendation from one of the people working there where I work with other members to write stories and brainstorm. We write short stories using prompts we come up with as a group and then share them during these group sessions. We collaborate on group writing projects and share stories about our weeks and sometimes lives.

I have changed so much in the past ten years. I have discovered a bunch of passions. I am a storyteller, a writer, a gamer, and a reader. I love strategy, I find a wide range of subjects intriguing, and I love to learn.

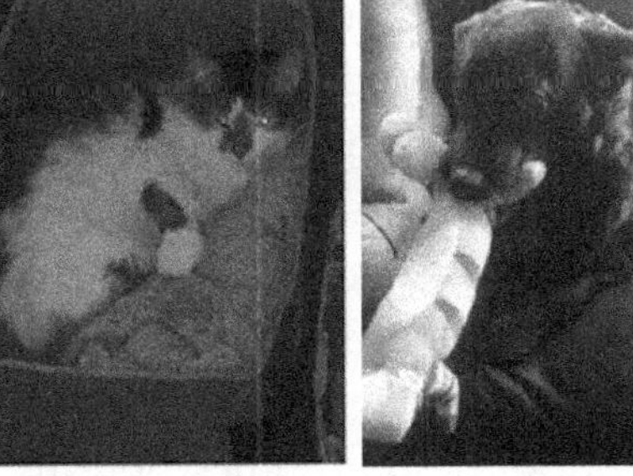

Questions of Spirituality
By Robert Williams

I began to realize that I could actually do things a little differently—leave my old life behind and start a new one. I moved out of my old town into the current town I'm now in, and I began building friendships. I began my journey to rewrite my life. I realized what things were important and left behind the things that were not. The important things included my family, and what they wanted me to achieve. I saw that, and I began to believe in myself in a new way. Instead of being where everything felt repressive, I am now in a place where I can feel safe. I can be safe and bring forth my talent into the world.

There was a time when I was very disapproving of people and didn't know how to regain my trust in the world. I knew what to look for, and even though I was a very sensitive, some might say I'm an HSP or highly-sensitive person. I am also someone who knows how to judge myself diplomatically, and I believe that there is a higher good watching over me.

In this town where I had started over, I met the love of my life: Heather. We supported each other very successfully—up to the point where I knew I needed to somehow discontinue the medication I was taking and move towards a natural means of getting better. This attempt had failed.

For a time, I thought I had lost everything forever: my partner, my family, and my trust in myself. I entered a new dark era, but these were my beliefs. I believed in the dark, but I didn't believe in the light and, yet, behind the shadows, the light was there to protect me and make me new again. It was then that I knew there were things that needed to change. I needed to change my health, so that meant I had to look at what I ate, my fitness level, and many different things that could ensure my revival, survival, and ability to thrive in the future.

My partner and I, even though we were not together, we both knew that we loved each other. It was written in the sand. There is a bond and a love that touched something within me that doesn't usually happen in humanity. And when it does, it gets misunderstood, abused, and misused. I knew she would be the one somewhere in the back of my mind.

After going to the hospital and having a mental breakdown, she was very stressed about my state of being and was by my side to help me through the process. Even though our relationship was teetering, she was there, and she knew that if the process was so stressful for her, it was worse for me. She also knew just how special it was to learn through this process on her own as well as learn beside me.

I was there in the hospital going through things that were so dark I never thought my mind could regenerate after that. My fears and darkness were beyond limitless. I didn't know how to support myself, and there were no supports around me. I didn't know how to support myself, what to ask for. And being as low as I was on my medication, there were no supports, as I was already on the medication they said I needed. I looked inside myself and found that nothing would work except calmness and being the only one in the room.

I know this sounds morbid, and I know it's probably a difficult read, but it's important to know what goes on behind the shadows because what's on the other side is very different. I knew things and felt things, and I thought I was the only one experiencing it. It's unbelievable the terror that I felt just being on my own with nobody else in the room, and yet it was the only time when I had some time to just be. It was a large, lengthy experience, my path towards healing, and at the end of it, I was getting better, so I continued. The main thing I needed was her, my former partner and now main support, who was there on the sidelines to help me. Yes, she was not my partner, but she was helping me in a pure way, as someone who cares and wants to be there for me.

Fast forward to a year later. I had begun my transformation and was dead set on becoming more for myself and more for Heather. These were the two main things that propelled me, as well as my family. I knew now that nutrition was extremely important, so I turned to a program called Nutritional Balancing. A healthcare professional who has partnered with other healthcare professionals and continues to do the work to improve her skills and improve what she does led him. Nutritional Balancing started with studying regimen, supplements, saunas, and diet (including things in the diet that one would not normally eat in order) to make the path towards slow oxidation.

For people who have not studied this or know much about it, Nutritional Balancing is a way to balance minerals and balance energy levels in such a way that allows the body to be in perfect symbiosis and in good health, along with lowering heavy metals in the system.

Now, this process went on for three years. Me and my partner were in and out of a relationship. It was only because of my struggle and my imbalance in myself and my judgments of myself, especially the inner work that I was yet to accomplish. There are so many ways in which human life feels rigorous, empty, hopeless, and void of what I consider a relationship with not just myself, but my spiritual self. This program allowed me to do some very interesting things, one of which was taking saunas. I would do saunas at least three times a week for at least an hour each time. Doing this coupled with the supplement regimen allowed me to start cleaning my body.

When I say cleaning my body, I mean really taking out the things that shouldn't be there, toxins that have built up over time, or heavy metals which come from food, drinking water, and exposure to pollution. I realized that there are very many things out there that didn't serve my best interest to keep me healthy.

This whole process of getting healthy was to eliminate the things that held me back. But the real work that came, that I realized I had no idea was there, was the inner work and the spiritual work combined. A year after completing my Nutritional Balancing program, I became a Reiki Master Teacher. I realized that I couldn't ignore the parts of me that were spiritual any longer. I had to incorporate them, pay attention to them, and nurse them into good health. Something I would recommend for many in the spectrum, as their high sensitivity may be just a sign that they are highly skilled empaths, simply seeking guidance and renewal, and to follow their dreams to help others and humanity move to the next stage.

This woman that is in my life now, whose name is Heather, was someone who lifted me up when I was in my worst stages and worst mental breakdowns. I have had few mental breakdowns in my life, but when they happened, they were notable and the worst experiences that I can remember. There is a lighter side to all this, however, which is, in hindsight, the pain and all the things endured actually made me stronger and also gave me things to learn.

Hard lessons usually show up in my life, but then, how many people does that not happen to? And do those people get to have the fruitful lessons the way they were and to the degree of learning that I have? These are big questions, and I know that I don't have all the answers, but I know I have a few, and I know that they have burned in like nothing else.

Now that I have my Reiki Master Teacher certification, I have been doing distance Reiki for clients for the last four years. I have to say that the success I've had there has proven to me the importance of just how much spirituality is an important endeavour for not just me, but for everyone in some way and somehow. All it takes is thinking. Thinking is not just thinking to me. It's a compass. It's a compass that points us in a direction. And that compass is not far from magical, but closest to being very understood, or non-understood, or unconsciously understood. And when I mean unconsciously understood, it's that we remark on it, and we use it all the time, but we fail to recognize its significance and how much it pertains to our own spirituality and that alone.

Even though our actions seem physical and electrical, they are also guided by a force that we do not yet comprehend. I have channeled energy to help a few people and they keep coming back to me for help. I consider this a big success, and I encourage those who also have these innate abilities who are struggling through life, thinking that everyone is just not a match for them.

I try to remember that these people and everyone are on their own journey to learn more about the things that they have repressed, denied, or failed to recognize. I know when I failed to recognize, I would make judgments, not only of myself, but of my partner and those close to me. And I would believe that, hell, it must be karma coming back to bite me in the you-know-what. Well, karma was the first hint. Karma could be the beginning of my spiritual journey. Because unfairness became karma, and karma became my own personal gain and my understanding of spirituality.

Sporting Chances
By Elliot Smith

Most of my interests are to do with sports, even my job is related to Sports Management! Since I was a young kid, I loved playing on sports teams, but it was really hard finding a team that would accommodate me. Well, I am going to tell you a story that shows how, with the right people and the right accommodations, a kid like me became an international sports celebrity!

I am currently involved with several leagues, and they are:

- Durham Region Challenger Baseball League,
- Greater Durham Special Olympics,
- Durham Eagles Softball Club,
- Pickering FC Learn to Train Advanced All Abilities League,
- Oshawa Vikings Mixed Ability Rugby League, and
- Mixed Ability Archery at Archery 2 You in Oshawa.

I am involved with these leagues because I am a committed athlete. I work hard every day to become successful to stay healthy and fit too. I like being a part of these teams because I can keep stimulated when I am trying to focus on being positive when playing sports. Mixed Ability Sports is where players with and without disabilities play on the same team regardless of age, ability, gender, race, or culture. It is where everyone is treated the same and everyone is welcome.

I play as a prop for the Oshawa Vikings Rugby League and have been playing in this league for 4 years now. I am also the Co-Captain of the Mixed Ability Rugby League. Our team has players of all ages and abilities including players from the Durham Lords Rugby League. My favourite sport is rugby, because I like the contact side, and I get to tackle and do it in a safe way. I also love making a good try (that is a score) and the teamwork is pretty incredible too.

What I like about rugby is that they make the majority of rugby pitches in the world accessible for people with disabilities. It's accessible because there are ways you can build a dream team by having rugby players with and without disabilities. Also, it is where everyone is treated the same, where everyone is included, and where everyone is welcome. Rugby helps me build self-confidence and teaches me how to make new friends on and off the field based on disability, age, gender, as well as cultural and religious background too. Our rugby club is very inclusive and accessible and is welcoming to all. The head coach, John Watkins is very understanding and takes the time to explain everything to me, breaks and letting me have breaks when I am feeling overstimulated.

I am very lucky to have been able to compete overseas. Never would I have thought I could play like this until I joined this team. I was picked on a lot as a young kid, and most kids would not pick me for their teams. They also would not give me any accommodations, so I had a really hard time with sports in school. I have overcome so much and broke those barriers down, and, now, I have played in two international tournaments overseas. I competed in Cork, Ireland in the International Mixed Ability Tournament in June of 2022, and our team came in second out of 17 other countries (and a total of 24 other teams).

I also was selected to be part of an elite team called the MARI Mixed Ability Rugby Invitational and was selected based on my ability and the fact that I have given so much back to the rugby community here in Canada. I went and played on a team with players from all over the world and played a tournament in Belfast, Ireland in May, 2023. The next big tournament we are playing in is the next World Cup in Pamplona, Spain in June, 2025, and we are training right now for it.

The rugby club is also very inclusive, and they let me build a sensory room with a grant I received from Autism Speaks Canada. It has lights, relaxing chairs, fidget toys, and lots of other sensory items. I use it almost every time I am there, and it helps me destress. The grant that I got was a $5,000 grant from Autism Speaks, where I built a sensory room for rugby players with disabilities to take a break from loud noises during practice or games or tournaments on the pitch. I did this because I wanted to tell rugby players that you can prevent yourself from having a meltdown if you are having a bad day playing rugby or if you need a break sometimes as well.

I have even written two children's books about my rugby experience called *Mateo's Mixed Ability Match* and *Elliot's Excellent MARI Match*. I wrote both books with my mom, and they are based on my international tournaments that I played in. We have used all sales to help make our Mixed Ability program bigger and better. A filmmaker also followed me around for a long time, and he made a documentary called Advantage Gained all about my rugby life. You can see the trailer on the website A New Story, check it out!

Being on this rugby team also helped me get a job at the Abilities Centre! I am a Physical Fitness and Literacy Associate, as well as a Mixed Ability Sports Facilitator and Coach. I go around to a lot of schools, colleges, and universities to talk about Mixed Ability Sport and to tell my sport story. This job has really helped my confidence and self-esteem.

The advice I would give to someone who wants to play rugby is that I would like to tell them to get active, go join a sports league such as Special Olympics, Mixed Ability Sport, or Jays Care Foundation, or MLSE Launchpad because then they would learn how to keep active. That would mean they would have to not give up on themselves, have a great group of support people, and learn that they are unstoppable. Also tell them they are not alone too because rugby is one of the few sports that are like family too!

Other Passions: Sandy & Casper

- Sandy is my eight-year-old rabbit. He is a lop ear rabbit. I love him and he cuddles with me. He is my therapy pet. He gets along with my Maine Coon cat really well.

- Casper is my Maine Coon cat, and he was adopted from the Humane Society. He is four years old now. I love him, and he purrs all the time.

SMART ASS JOKESTER & WRITER
BY JUSTIN HUMPHREYS

My name is Justin P. Humphreys and I am the author of some stories in the book you're reading currently. I am a smart-ass adult with autism. I am a member of Durham's Autism Home Base, and I love the friends and community I've found there. My interests include politics, comedy, guns, playing guitar, hunting, video games, and history. I am 28 and I like to spend time with friends, family and my dog, plus my mom's puppy. My favourite movie is *The Godfather Part 2*. My favourite food is steak.

Games & Cooking—My Favourite Things
By Eric Lauder

Like a good number of other guys my age (mid 20s), my favourite hobby is probably video games. I love them. I like Soulsborne games a fair bit, also Monster Hunter, Pokémon, and Shin Megami Tensei. I'm a big fan of games with a lot of potential for customization in regard to a character's equipment or a team's composition. I like a good story as much as the next guy, but I enjoy the freedom of making a build custom-tailored to suit my preferences and playstyle. I also enjoy the process of gradually getting stronger and fighting against bigger, scarier foes with new weapons and/or teammates, with style and power alike. Of course, I also like it when skill is involved, since games become boring if they're just numbers games; I like a little challenge, hence my love of the Souls series.

Sekiro is still one of my genuine favourites. My all-time favourite series probably remains Monster Hunter though. Perhaps mentioned elsewhere, I have an innate love for seeking patterns and manipulating AI. Every game is made up of code, and AI is simply a part of that code, dictating how enemies and non-player characters act in any given situation. It can be simple or complex, depending on the game.

In terms of Monster Hunter, all the monsters have AIs that dictate how they fight against the player. It is best discussed in terms of "movesets": every different enemy has different attacks that serve some purpose, with the ultimate goal of defeating the player. Sometimes the goal is to deal damage or create some space to stop the player from attacking or some other purpose. The point being, each of these moves have a specific use within the fight. Knowing these functions, and the factors surrounding their use, combined with other factors such as distance, health, status, etc., one can accurately predict when a certain move is going to come out, and how best to avoid it, granting windows of opportunity for counter-attacks. Long story short, I love disassembling AI within video games. It isn't just another world, it's one where everything is rooted in some definitive, numerical logic, which can be understood and exploited with enough effort.

I also have some love of cooking! Granted, I don't have much choice, being the de facto chef of the household, but I do like to experiment with recipes now and again. Meatloaf is one of my most common, being moderately quick and easy, but I have made other, more exciting recipes before, as well! Two that stand out in particular are my Japanese-style curry (which I didn't include as my favourite recipe in this book because it has to simmer for about three to four hours, but it was delicious! Also had chocolate in it, which sounds weird, but still yummy!) and my fusion-style Korean fried cauliflower, which is a pain to prepare, requiring one to both make a sauce from scratch and fry cauliflower in a pot of oil, which can get painful if done incorrectly. Like with the video games, I enjoy the customizability of cooking, where any recipe can be tweaked or altered in order to fit one's mood or preference. It's also a fairly straight-forward, logical venture, where everything just kinda makes sense, which is one of the reasons I find it kinda relaxing.

Gamer Girl from the UK
By Ciara Freeman

Everyone has hobbies! Everyone has a passion that excites them, be it painting, movies, golf… autistic people tend to take these passions to another level. I was four years old when I picked up the controller for the original Xbox, kickstarting a hyper fixation that would never leave me. I'm a nerd, and I always have been. Growing up, most girls wanted to talk about horses, or High School Musical, when I'd be bursting to tell absolutely anyone about my encyclopedic knowledge of the latest video games that had captured my attention.

I started gaming on my parents' Xbox, and sometimes my dad would download a few games on his PC too. I grew up playing a lot of Elder Scrolls, Oddworld, and Fable. I adored immersing myself into these fantastical and whimsical settings. When I was six years old, I got the Nintendo Wii for Christmas, and my fixation for gaming grew even deeper. I remember always rushing to turn on my Wii the second I got home from school every day; I absolutely loved the thing! I struggled to communicate or make friends at school, so after a long day of feeling like a weird little alien in a world not built for me, coming home to play games was my escape. I had all of these different worlds to run away to where my social skills didn't matter. I didn't have to mask or pretend to be "normal," I didn't have to be scared of people, because the people on my screen were just pixels. Nobody inside of these games would judge me or think I'm weird, gaming gave me a space where I could just be me.

As the years went on, I still spent almost all of my free time gaming. Then Minecraft was released. Minecraft was and still is a hugely popular game, but something about it was especially appealing to autistic people. Having full control of your own blocky world, building everything your mind can think of—it was the kind of escape that many autistic people were needing. It was so easy to become completely immersed in it.

Minecraft was the first ever online game I had played, which meant I could join servers and message with the people I was playing with. Meeting other autistic people my age through Minecraft really helped me, because I didn't know any other autistic people locally at that point. I would spend hours every day playing Minecraft and making friends with people that actually understood me.

Then I discovered live streaming. Having the ability to be able to stream any game to a live audience opened up many more opportunities for me to make friends. I still wasn't able to make friends at school, and by this point, my school life was severely affecting my mental health in a negative way. Every single day after I came home from school, I would start up a game, start livestreaming it, and play with my audience for as long as I could. These were the only times during my days where I wouldn't feel so lonely, and I have gaming to thank for that. Eventually this small audience would grow into a community of people, and with the help of my new cozy community, I started live-streaming for charity. I would stay up for 24 hours, streaming Minecraft to raise funds for a chosen charity.

Over the years, 24 hours became 48, then 72 hours. What started as small streams alone in my bedroom, became large marathons with a team of people behind them, hosted from an office space hours away from my home. The last event was hosted in 2020, just before the pandemic hit. Nowadays, I don't get the time to be able to regularly host these marathons, but I'd love to return to it one day.

I'm now twenty-four, and I still play games daily, for as long as I can get away with, while juggling the tasks that adulthood throws at me. Gaming isn't as much of a social outlet for me now, but I now have a decent social life offline and don't have the same need for that outlet as I did in my teenage years.

I think many people judged my parents for letting me play games as much as I did growing up, and sure, I get it. But what people don't understand is how much of a lifeline gaming was for me. It allowed me to develop socially when school was holding me back in that regard, and it gave me an escape when I couldn't handle the events of the real world any longer. My lifelong special interest in gaming is a large part of why I am who I am today.

PART 3:
INDEPENDENCE

Conversation About Independence

WE TALKED
REDEFINING INDEPENDENCE
AUTISTIC VOICES ON SELF-SUFFICIENCY, SUPPORT, AND THE FREEDOM TO CHOOSE

KATHERINE: What I want for myself in terms of independence is just around self-sustaining things. Like, I can cook my own meals and that if I need to: I can live far away from my parents. Honestly just basic things–it doesn't necessarily need to be so deep. Just taking care of myself.

The way that my parents would refer to it is common sense, but that isn't necessarily what it is.

I guess with cooking, when you're frying something in a pan, and you leave the pan, what you're meant to do or what's safe to do is you tilt the handle of the pan back towards the stove so someone doesn't knock it off the stove. I never thought of that. And I think that's just because I don't usually think of stuff like that. I don't think that makes sense to do because, in my head, it's just I was never instructed to do it. So I guess it's little safety stuff like that.

I'm planning on being in college by next September, so I'll be living in a dorm, and I won't have my parents at all.

AKOSUA: And I know Corey, you've got a unique situation where you got your whole family around you in a way, although you have your own place.

COREY: Yeah, I have my own apartment, pay my own bills, all that fun stuff. My mom lives across the hallway in her own place with her boyfriend. My brother lives directly across the hall in his own place. And then my uncle lives downstairs. So, I have a good chunk of my immediate family in the building. My health is getting pretty crap, and right now I'm currently trying to get a lot of supports, but there's only so much that can be done.

But on the days where the pain in my legs is so bad that I can't even physically stand up, my mom will help me with my dog and stuff. My mom helps me with cooking balanced meals cuz the most I can really do is quick and easy stuff because just leaning over a sink to do dishes, I get a tension in my spine that feels like it's bending in a way that it shouldn't, and it starts in my legs and goes all the way up my spine, right?

I'm requiring a cane for balance. I got a walker within the last month, and I'm currently getting supports installed in my apartment: a rail for the shower, something to help me get in and out of bed in the morning and the evening, and then something to raise the toilet seat because it's a low flush toilet.

AKOSUA: So, it doesn't seem like autism is one of the reasons you need support. There's so many other things.

COREY: Unfortunately, I was cursed with a lot more than autism. I also have schizo affective disorder and the physical things with my legs. Those are the main reasons I need help right now.

So independence for me is having my freedom of choice. I spent my entire childhood and teen years having that taken away from me on a regular basis. Didn't even get to choose the clothes I wore on my back.

So just having my freedom of choice is independence for me.

BRIANNA: Being able to make my own choices is important to me, too. I live with my mom, and she helps with my son, and I am so glad I have her support and other supports, too. Being able to do daily tasks independently and supporting myself is why I feel independent.

SCOTT: I wanted to add to what Corey said. Independence needs a group. I live with my friends, and I go to work, and I have this group, the writing group. If I was completely alone, I don't know what would have happened. You need connection so that you can be independent.

AKOSUA: You mentioned that you work in a factory, and that gives you the money you need and allows you to do whatever you want in a way as your work doesn't take up all your mental space.

SCOTT: Work is an assembly line: simple, repetitive and—for me—kind of soothing in a way. And it gives me time to think about stories.

AKOSUA: Elliot, you took a course on independent living at college. How did that set you up for more independence?

ELLIOT: Independence means I can get groceries for my mom at the grocery store which is right across from our apartment. I can take the bus on my own to work out. I have a part-time job as a physical fitness and literacy associate and mixed ability sport facilitator at the Ability Center in Whitby. I can play sports without support at the Vikings Rugby Club or any other sports league in the community that I play at. And I also can go out for walks on my own and sometimes I use the apartment gym when it's too cold or too hot out.

AKOSUA: Wow, that's a very full life.

ELLIOT: I'm very active, and I also went to college so I could live in residence with my roommate that lives in Whitby, and his family's from

Jamaica. He was a very good roommate to me for two years in Fleming College in Peterborough.

AKOSUA: What kind of courses did you take that helped you with independence?

ELLIOT: Mostly an international culinary lab, like a foods around the world business course. I had to learn about the travel industry and did a project on where I was going to visit and whatnot. I got to learn about how to make progress with friends at college and also about first aid and CPR. I was learning how to have safe sex relationships and learning how to cook meals from scratch. I learned how to take transit to my co-op placement and to take transit to the Peterborough sport and wellness center. Sometimes I didn't even take the city transit bus at all. Sometimes I walked there because it was within walking distance to my residence.

AKOSUA: That course sounds amazing.

ELLIOT: Yeah! It was very brilliant.

AKOSUA: Owen isn't here today, but in one of his articles, he mentioned that, in the Autism Room, he did a project where he had to create a budget for life after school. I don't think a lot of the other classes talk about making budgets. I know they're talking a lot about financial literacy in schools now as it's a skill most people should have, but he only got it because he was part of that special ed class.

He wrote that in his class, they were talking about living with a disability. He called it Poverty 101 as he felt they were trying to teach him how to live a crap life. He wrote in the book how as part of the budget, he was researching the cost of owning a car and the teaching assistant and the teacher were saying, "Haven't you learned anything in this course? You won't be able to afford a car because you are disabled."

But he knew better as he was working throughout high school. His happiest moment was when he got a car before he graduated–he should have driven over his teacher's toes! Just kidding!

ALL: [Laughter]

[…]

AKOSUA: Mhm.

[…]

ALL: [Laughter]

[…]

Akosua: One of the stats I've heard is disturbing because we all need money to live and that in the autism community, the unemployment rate is as high as 80 percent. Have others found difficulties getting jobs? I know that Justin H. has been looking for a job for years and others who are in this group have mentioned that as well.

[...]

Akosua: Elliot, your mom told us about when they made an accommodation for you so you could keep one earbud in and in that way keep your job.

Elliot: Yes, with one earbud in the ear rather than using both. That's because I have to listen to my radio on the job to make sure if someone needs assistance I can help them. For example, if someone needs an incident report filled out, then it has to be written on file because if someone gets hurt, I have to do first aid or CPR, if someone passes out or has a collapse or has a heart attack or something. They usually have to be rushed to the hospital to make sure they get checked out to make sure nothing's bad happened to them. The one earbud helps me because then I can listen to my music and then I can listen to what communications I can hear on my radio, on my talkie, at the same time. My music helps me relax. With one bud in, I can still hear if other staff or my supervisor need assistance...

Wayman: My device that allows me to hear. It connects to my hearing aids.

Akosua: Cool. So technology helps.

Wayman: I'm very dyslexic and I guess I didn't really learn to read properly until very late in life. I could still read, but then I'd have to start to read again. Just the processing doesn't work. Language processing. It's the same with hearing accents. I don't get them at all.
People who speak quickly? I can't process language quickly. And it's not that it's a hearing problem, it's a processing problem.

I worked in The Royal Canadian Air Force as a communication technician. In electronics.

Scott: Cool.

Akosua: How did you choose the air force?

Wayman: I was trying to get through high school, and I never did get it completed. So I'm still missing a subject or two. But to get beyond that, I went, and I applied for air crew, and they sent me to air crew selection, and I washed out of that because I wear glasses, and I think it's a deficit to wear glasses when you're flying a fighter aircraft! Understandable. So I went back in and actually joined the Air Force, and, through selection, I got into electronics communications, and I worked in that the whole time I was there.

It was a very broad category of communications and ground support. You have anything from inter-office communication gadgets to microwave communications. I was in Moose Jaw, Saskatchewan for my first posting. That's a pilot training base. Interesting. They had very tough aircrafts to survive what student pilots put those aircrafts through.

AKOSUA: And then you found work helping people with dyslexia, and you mentioned nonverbal autistic kids.

WAYMAN: That all happened after I left the Air Force. I decided I needed to get some sort of education to be able to get a job. So I went to university and the very first thing we had to do in psych class was to analyze our own study habits. So I documented them quite thoroughly and handed it in. The TA that got it said, "I'm not doing anything with that," and passed it on to the Professor who looked at it and called me into his office.

He said, "You got to be kidding. This is not how it works!" and I said, "That's how it works for me." And he said, "We'll send you over to Student Aid."

And then at Student Aid I participated in a study–a lady there was doing her doctorate on learning disabilities. I don't know how many tests people here have taken, but there were a huge number of tests and the bottom line of them all was that something's not right.

I tested at the top of the spectrum, and I tested at the bottom of the spectrum. So I was sent off away from the campus for some specialized testing. One was testing audio response and part of the problem is that I have a missing or delayed P300.

I think it is what would cue me to what's happening around me, but it's missing. So if I start to do work and focus on something, the world around me disappears. If somebody wants to talk to me, they would have to touch me to cue me into their environment.

The result of the testing was diagnosing that I'm dyslexic. How they found that, despite that fact I have an extremely highly developed coping mechanism… I was 30 years old at that point in time. So, I'd had a lifetime filled up of coping and allowing myself to disappear and things. But, how they caught me after days of testing, was they said, "We don't know, but we've got this one last test we want to try." It was a sheet of foolscap with one line after another typed on it and they told me to copy it all as quickly as I could.

The first line of copying was pretty good. The next line was starting to get iffy. By the third or fourth line, it was jibberish. They stopped me. They said, "Okay, we know what's the trouble." Great. What is it? "You're very dyslexic." My question, what can I do about it? The answer: We don't know. That answer really destroyed me.

[…]

WAYMAN: I very very strongly developed coping mechanisms in school right from get-go. My grade one teacher was a terror. I tried to get my parents to arrange with the teacher for some extra tutoring because I just wasn't coping with anything in the class, but that fell off almost instantly. So I muddled my way through. I learned how to disappear in a class.

KATHERINE: That's like me in grade school! I was diagnosed with autism, I think around six or seven, and they started putting me in specialized classes and such. And I found that I absolutely detested the feeling of being pandered to and the feeling that my independence or whatever might be taken away. So, I started rejecting the diagnosis and throughout most of grade school and high school, I completely rejected that I was autistic. And I found that I developed coping mechanisms through not using my IEP. I stopped using it. I essentially tried to prove to them I wasn't autistic.

And for jobs, I found that the most effective way to sustain a job would be if I just completely masked my autism, just entirely, if I could. I can't fully because that's impossible, but that's what I did. And I've maintained jobs by completely masking it. Completely and as effectively as I can, I try to act neurotypical. So I don't know if that's entirely an independence piece, but it was sort of myself asserting my own independence.

[…]

KATHERINE: 100%. I feel awful. I feel gross. I want to puke. I don't feel good when I mask. But also, I don't want to be neurotypical, but I want to be successful, and that's not to say that someone with autism can't be successful, but a lot of the time with the way that our world is organized, it is assumed that if you're autistic, you can't be independent, you can't be successful. I want to live on my own, and I want to fully be on my own because I want to prove to people that I can.

[…]

WAYMAN: Just to mention very very early in life, from what I hear from what people have said anyways, I fit not into anything. So I was unable to cope with the world around me, with people. And my mother used to tie me to the chair so that I would stop moving while I was trying to have supper or something like that. Just needing to move is still with me. I cover it now by just moving my feet and my toes. They're always in motion.

AKOSUA: So that's your strategy.

ERIC: I mean, yeah, independence is a real issue for me cuz I guess I'm just not quite sure where I fit. At some level, I am independent but at the same time, I have people who depend on me, and I depend on them in turn. So it's a real give and take type situation.

A lot of people have said this before, but, I mean, there's just this thing, right, where you tell people about your disability and suddenly people start treating you like a kid or start acting like you're stupid or you can't understand anything. And it's just frustrating because it's like, yeah, I have a disability, but that doesn't mean I don't have the capacity to work or be intelligent or be independent…

[…]

Independence—What Does It Mean When You Have Disabilities? By Ciara Freeman

The journey to independence often looks a little different for autistic people. I think everyone has their own unique view of what "being independent" really means. For me, independence is having my own peace, preparing and eating the food I've chosen, having the freedom to drive. By my own definition, I'm not independent, or at least not yet.

As well as being autistic, I have other disabilities that have forced me to change my perspective of independence. I get significantly more chronically exhausted than other people, and my immune system is very low. Illnesses hit me harder and take me a lot longer to fully recover. My health is very unpredictable day to day, which leaves me in the position of not being able to work a regular job. I'm sure a lot of other people's definitions of independence include working a stable job, mine doesn't.

This doesn't mean I don't work, but I've had to go different routes to get where I want to be, to try and achieve my definition of independence. I remember when I was very young and in school, a teacher was trying to teach me how to read. I was having none of it—my parents read to me! Why should I need to learn how to read if my parents can read to me? The teacher asked me what if my parents weren't around one day when I needed to read something? I replied, "Well, that's when I'll learn how to read!"

For better or for worse, that's kind of the attitude I've held throughout my life. My parents always took very good care of me, and considering my ill health held me back from taking care of myself a lot—it's what I needed. However, this also meant that I didn't learn how to do a lot of things for myself. By 2020, my health had started very gradually improving to the point I could start leaving the house more, which was pretty exciting, as I've always been fairly housebound for the most part. Then the first COVID-19 lockdown hit. My mother had just begun a new job somewhere she was at a higher risk of getting infected, and my immune system was too bad to risk getting COVID from her, so I moved in with my new boyfriend only a few months after we met.

I generally thought I was pretty independent by that point. I mean, I can get a bus by myself, what more do I need to learn? Well, I was thrown into the deep end. Overnight my life became a slurry of washing up, paying bills, and doing my taxes. This is the dreaded "adulthood" I've heard so much about huh? I hadn't been taught how to do these things before. The same attitude I had about reading all those years ago came back to bite me in the ass. Now I need to learn fifty new things just to keep myself alive and sane.

My boyfriend helped me a lot; he showed me the ropes and he helped with the things I couldn't handle sometimes due to my health. I guess that's what my idea of independence became: simply trying my best. So that's what I've been doing in my years of new-found adulthood. My sensory issues forbid me from washing dishes because foam is my personal idea of hell. I have three different clothing piles at all times: one for clean clothes, one for unclean clothes, and the pile for clothes that aren't clean but also aren't unclean enough to be washed again yet. Learning to drive means being trapped in a 1-1 interaction for an hour while overanalyzing an even larger environment, so that's on the to do later list.

For the most part, I feel very positively about being autistic, but I can't lie and say that it's not disabling for me either. I couldn't wash my own hair until I was twenty-two years old because again, foam is my personal idea of hell. My teeth aren't fantastic because brushing my teeth equals foam, and y'know, that's just hell, except inside my mouth, not to mention, who on earth decided putting strong mint flavours inside these tubes of foamy hell equals being more hygienic?

Becoming independent wasn't so much about overcoming these things and just "getting over it." It is more about finding ways to make the unbearable a little bit more bearable. I've had to find toothpaste and shampoo that doesn't foam as much, a dishwasher is a must, and sometimes I have to ask for help. My best isn't exactly what I pictured being independent would look like, but it works for me, and I'm proud to have gotten myself this far.

Searching For Employment—Becoming A Chef
By Justin Humphreys

The search for employment has been over two years now without success with getting employment, but still no desire to quit. I'd rather continue my search for employment than give up. Having independence is something I desire above all. I've been applying for jobs on the job site Indeed. Recently, I had a job interview, but I didn't get it; however, I am hopeful that I will get the job in the future. I would like to one day have my own restaurant and do a menu inspired by Dahmer for Halloween.

Tourtiere Recipe Learned in College
By Justin Humphreys

Prepare Tourtiere Filling

Meat filling

1 large cooked peeled quartered russet potato (reserve the water)
1 teaspoon salt
1 teaspoon butter
1 large finely-chopped onion
1 pinch salt
1/2 cup finely diced celery
1 pound ground beef
1 pound ground pork
1 cup of potato cooking water

Sautée the ground beef and ground pork then mix with the spice blend below:

SPICE BLEND

2 teaspoons of salt
1 teaspoon of ground black pepper
1/2 teaspoon dried sage
1/2 teaspoon ground cinnamon
1/2 teaspoon ground ginger
1/4 teaspoon allspice
1/4 teaspoon grated nutmeg
1/4 teaspoon ground mustard
1/8 ground cloves
1 pinch cayenne.

PREPARE CRUST

3 cups of all-purpose flour
2 sticks of frozen unsalted butter sliced
1 teaspoon of salt
7 teaspoons of cold water
2 teaspoons of distilled white vinegar

Stir wet ingredients and mix dry ingredients separately, then combine and add flour.

Roll using a rolling pin.

Preheat oven to 400°.

Once dough is rolled, place it into a foil shell—use fork to seal edges and trim excess off pie shell.

Add filling and cover with dough.

Make egg wash and brush pie shell plus cut slits in the top of pie shell.

Place tourtiere in the preheated oven for 35-40 mins.

Serve tourtiere while still warm.

MAY AS WELL HOPE
BY OWEN BRYAN

Content Warning: Suicidal Ideation, Discussions on Medication,
Conspiracy Theories

Hi, I'm Owen, and I am 29. I am dreading that my birthday is only nine days away as then I'll be OLD. I will be thirty. I was hoping to have financial independence and so much more by now.

I was born in England and grew up in Canada. I am in Canada at the moment, but I am considering moving to somewhere else to escape the life I made for myself. It feels like because of the events I'm going to tell you about in this story and because of the choices I made in response to them, I have backed myself into a corner that now leaves me with few good options. I've created a situation here that is so bad that I don't think it has a chance to improve unless I leave and start again. I'm thinking about moving to Detroit, Michigan for a few months to be able to rent a house more affordably, based on what I've seen online. They also have really cheap land houses there—many houses that are in very bad shape. With my skills, maybe one day I could renovate an entire house. Building or renovating a house is something that I always wanted to do. It is a dream of mine.

Doing this means I could even have a big house. I've seen some five-bedroom homes with nice yards that appear to be within my budget in Detroit—yes, I know it is a dangerous area, but I'd stick to myself and build a high fence and secure garage for my car. It would be extremely difficult to even rent a house that size here on a single income, and I do not want to spend my life renting small spaces. I'm also considering other places like Namibia in Africa. I'm looking at the economic conditions of places in Mexico. We have a few family friends who have created lives there. Our neighbours are from Namibia, and I've done a lot of research about the life I could afford if I moved there.

I just feel so beaten down by all these things that have happened to me, that all I want to do is go somewhere far away, build myself a nice place to live with a bit of land around me and to be left alone. Stay away from people. I don't want to be forced into a smaller life, to have roommates, and I've given up on new friendships. Realistically, no way in hell I'd ever have a romantic relationship. If any of that was going to happen, then at my age, it already would have.

To be honest, my vision of my future here is terrifying to me. I just feel like it can't be good. So, it's clearly my best option to start again—to find and build a homestead and spend the rest of my life there. I'm practically at the point of hoping to experience a sudden death, like a heart attack, car accident, or something as soon as I tire of the hermit life. The difficult and confusing thing is that I have noticed that the act of researching and striving, and the thought of actively building and maintaining a new life away from this one, is reducing my boredom and dissatisfaction.

Weird, eh?

Additionally, I've been working with a career coach who has significantly helped me. He's helped me find a subject area that I like and where the jobs could fit a person like me—someone not good at socializing. So, I'm actively trying to get skills and experience in digital marketing. Although I couldn't finish college earlier, I'm now close to completing an online certificate. I am getting straight 90s. I've even lined up my first three customers.

I am in the middle of a hypnosis program at the moment, and I'm looking into my options to improve my nutrition. I go out for walks with my stepdad and his dogs, and I talk to my mom. I am trying to read self-help books, as my mom has a lot of book recommendations. I just don't want to try medication as my stomach is sensitive. Once, when I took medication, it made me nauseous, and I couldn't eat. I'm not willing to risk that. I believe that Big Pharma is a threat. I don't want to be reliant on medication the rest of my life, so I won't start that. I've tried it before, and I always forget to take it anyway.

So, this shows I am trying to improve things. But the motivation is tough to hang on to. It is tiny and fleeting. I try although I remain convinced that I can't escape, ending up with a life I will hate as much as the one I have now. But it is clear I haven't given up as I'm still here, despite how much I rage and gripe about it. How much I think about MAID (if you are in Canada, you know what that is—Medical Assistance in Dying). Giving up is harder than I thought, so for now, all I can do is keep going.

~*~

Autism has been a feature of the most negative aspects of my life and does not feel like something I would ever embrace. From my perspective, I feel my struggles have more to do with the loss of my father and all the chaos that followed, rather than actually having autism. In fact, the first time the idea was floated that I had autism, it was by an expert witness for the defense in the court proceedings following the drunk driving crash that killed my dad. The insurance company was the defence. Their lawyer argued that the court shouldn't award me that much money because, since I was autistic, my life would suck anyway!

After the accident, looking back, it was like pure chaos when what I needed more than ever was peace and the space to heal. Things, such as my primary caregiver (my mom) also being deeply affected by that event, and then not long afterwards, me struggling in a family situation that didn't suit me at all. I cannot get into that now, because that in itself could fill a book. Besides the crash and the family situation, we were constantly moving. In high school alone, I spent each grade in a different school, finally spending the last 1.5 years at the school I ended up graduating from.

But my struggles and the resulting trauma have many parallels with the autistic experience. Are compounded by it. I was told by my grandma that I seemed to be completely different to this as a young child before the accident. Me and my dad had a special bond until he died when I was 2.5 years old. When he died, I lost a part of myself as well. I've been heartbroken ever since. And now my beloved grandmother, who I could always talk to, has Alzheimer's. I've tried to move forward the best I could. I guess I unravelled in the aftermath of the loss of my dad. And then entering school amid all this made it worse. I haven't made the progress I expected to make in my 20s and losing my grandmother is feeling like more than I can handle.

One thing I noticed at school was that it was not a safe place for anyone different. As a kid with the issues that I had, I guess I felt safer not engaging, because it seemed like it was better to be the quiet kid than to open my mouth and worry that I'd instead be a weird/different kid that would be a target of bullying and harassment. I witnessed bullying frequently. At least as the quiet kid, people completely ignored my existence instead of harassing me. This helped in that I was not frequently a target of bullies—it seems I was mostly invisible to them—I was not worth the bother. But being ignored by bullies and everyone else made me feel I was of little value. Most other people at school, including the bullies, had friends, and I did not. The fact that I had no one in my corner as soon as I stepped into the school building every day only increased my vulnerability, causing me to fall deeper into these protective behaviors meant to keep me safe. But I know they are part of why my life has been going from bad to worse.

I remember school being a pretty soul-crushing experience. I was the kid that scarcely said a word at school. That fact alone, the fact that I hardly felt comfortable enough there to say a single word, made it such a difficult place to be for the amount of time that I spent there. Many hours a day, five days a week, 18 long years of being at school, of traveling there and back. I just kept quiet.

Whatever I have been suffering from for the past while, it is not something that I am in any way happy to have experienced. That saying "whatever doesn't kill you makes you stronger" is a stupid lie. Those things just make you want to kill yourself. The honest truth is that I regret surviving the accident that killed my father. I regret it every day. It's the first thought that pops into my mind in the morning and the last thing I think before finally getting to sleep. How much better off I would be if only I had died, too. Dying as a blank slate, rather than living long enough to bring shame and defeat to myself the way I have.

Furthermore, in society, I've heard people think there is a possibility of a world/society that is inclusive and where there is a place for everyone. But in my humble opinion, I don't see that at all. Being disabled is very scary. A disability requires a cold and uncaring world to change, and for it to make accommodations to support individuals with disabilities. I don't feel this society, this world, is safe, fair, or equitable. I have always considered there might be an environment like this out there, and it is what I need to recover my lost confidence. Everyone needs a few wins in this life.

Having lost my father, having no friends, and all the missing out that comes with that, plus the career issues, struggling to function, and having financial difficulties all feed into the sheer magnitude of my feelings of helplessness and despair. It has led to a negative outlook on life and my future. I now have a very "survival of the fittest" mentality. I see myself as someone who is on the wrong side of that. My confidence is on the floor. Being a loner with issues with communication, employment, and no friends makes me feel worthless. I don't even feel fully human, sitting in this corner with no real life. I am Black, and I remember learning that during slavery, slaves were considered 3/5 human. That's how I feel—like

I'm not fully human. I feel trapped in what feels like to me one of the most humiliating of loser-hood scenarios that has now exceeded my most pessimistic expectations. I am constantly asking, where does this end?

Another thing I didn't expect was how much of the things I thought I'd made peace with as a child suddenly come back with a vengeance as I get older. A future of being alone feels much more abstract when one is contemplating it as a child still in grade school, but now that I am almost thirty, that future almost feels like it's upon me and taking root. I am being ambushed by feelings that I thought I had made peace with. Turns out, all I did was sweep my problems under the rug. As a child, I remember that, yes, the pain of the failures in the social area really stung, but I tried to reason it away by thinking I could still find a career and that financial success would compensate. It's another long story, but work/career wise, I have also been stuck.

I know this story is very hard to read because of the negativity, but I haven't given up as I am still here. And in being here, in being around people like my mother, I sometimes do raise my head above my misery and push forward, even though the way my mind works, I am quick to bury myself in shit again.

Life is more brutal and difficult than I ever realized. It is just sink or swim. You either learn to function and find a place in the world, and a way of contributing, and enjoy the rewards that come from that. Or sink. I have been sinking for a long time. Am I too far gone? But I want you to know this and to look at those who are outside of society's care.

~*~

It is so hard, but I try. I definitely feel the time passing by, and the anxiety that comes with spending another second trapped in a life I hate. A second I won't get back. At times I can see that it is the seemingly small things that can make a day bearable. At times, I am hopeful that one day consistently using what I learned through hypnosis and this tapping method can help keep doom from invading my soul for a while. If I can do some things like in this list, I can have bearable days. I figure if I can make a poster of this list, it will remind me what to do when things get bad. Can these lead to more and more good days? Books and my mother say yes. I am less sure.

I like things like:
- Getting out of the house
- Hot showers and baths

- Being around family can distract you from the problems of life
- Helping my mom by cleaning up–I am great at this
- Spend a few minutes catching up with my brothers and sisters
- Joking around with my mother and brother
- Researching ways to improve things
- Cooking my own spicy food
- Learning new skills
- Buying tools that will be useful later
- Watching documentaries about useful things like people who have built small homesteads and documentaries about animals

I'm still here and I push through, although I fight it, as I just want to rest. I am just so tired of feeling worthless. Tired of having to carry all this self-hatred and despair. It's hard to imagine a future for myself that doesn't consist of being a struggling, bitter, lonely, and increasingly isolated person constantly wrestling with the dilemma of whether it is even worth it to continue living. Yes, the more life I lose to these feelings, the deeper it feels like despair pulls me in, and grips my arm and pulls me downwards. I used to think "it had better change by the time I'm thirty," but it hasn't.

Yet I am still here.

And with my family's support, I am working to develop a career. I might hope to have a life that is merely bad, not horrible, with some good days in it. I know I frustrate them. This morning, I became very upset with, things, and, when I calmed down, I understood there were other things I could have done instead of "go nuts." My mother and my brother who I live with, I know they love me even though I am hard to deal with at times when frustration overtakes me.

When I build my house and have nature, not people, around, I think it could be okay. I will want them to visit me, to come stay with me at times, though. Now I'm close to having qualifications and with clients lined up and the support of my career coach and my mother, I should soon be able to make enough money to cover my more basic needs to support myself. And then more. I want to make enough money to make it easier for my mother, as I know I've made it difficult for her. Maybe she'll come live in the woods with me. That would be ideal.

I want financial independence, life not to suck, and a house in the woods. And it's so hard to admit because it seems too painful to hope…

eventually I'd like friends… just a few. Maybe even a family, a child someday. It is hard to believe it's possible because of my past, but I am still here, so I may as well hope.

Spicy Ground Beef Recipe
By Owen Bryan

My family calls this "my favourite." I think it is more their favourite of all the things I cook. It is really simple and goes well with plain, white rice.

Ingredients

- Six spices: turmeric, cumin, chili powder, coriander, salt, pepper
- One large onion
- Two or three cloves of garlic
- A pound of ground beef
- Oil for sautéing
- About a quarter cup of frozen peas (optional)

Chop the onion and the garlic.

Sautée them in a pan with olive oil.

Once the onion is translucent, add the spices and keep stirring. You can add one teaspoon of each, except for the chili. One teaspoon is probably too much—so I'd suggest only a quarter of a teaspoon of chilli.

Add the ground beef to the spicy onions and garlic. I use a potato masher to mash the ground beef as it cooks.

You can tell it is done when the ground beef has no pink in it. Then leave it to cook for five or ten more minutes so you are sure the ground beef is well cooked through.

It tastes delicious with rice. This makes enough to feed our whole family of five. If you have less people to serve, that is great because it tastes even better warmed up as leftovers. If you are adding the frozen peas, it is good to add them after the ground beef is cooked (has no pink in it).

A Personal Experience with Dyslexia
By Wayman Edward Sole

This is based in part on my presentation at a panel discussion, on 27 November, 1996, Facilitated by Janet Ackland, Resource Counsellor for the Learning Disabilities Association, London Middlesex.

Although I am dyslexic, I hadn't begun to understand what this meant until very recently [fall, 1991]. Historically, my academic record was poor and recent forays into formal education have had mixed results. I have found that what I do to support dyslexia also helps autistic traits. I have learned from my own experiences as well as through formal training how to help others like me. That extends to nonverbal, non-social children.

A Quick Look at Growing Up

From birth, I was equipped with a world view that differed significantly from the accepted norm. I did not relate well to others or with my environment, and early school was more akin to a place of fear and confusion than a place for fun and learning. And yes, it was also a place to do battle with teachers. But, doing battle didn't help, so I gradually developed a set of survival skills—some may say coping skills—that allowed me to figuratively disappear in a classroom. My thought was, if I don't say or do anything to attract attention, then perhaps nobody would pay any attention to me. This worked remarkably well, except that, in doing so, I separated myself from much needed help. Whatever the reason, I was a poor scholastic achiever and many of my elementary and high school report cards carried the phrases "not performing up to potential," "an underachiever," or similar comments.

At home, my parents taught us acceptable social skills and self-discipline from a very early age. In my case, this process was at times a battle of wills. Fortunately, my parents accepted this and continued to encourage me to put forth my best effort.

Looking back, I now realize my parents always made sure I was challenged to succeed within whatever bounds seemed to exist. For example, mechanical building bits and a number of clocks and watches to dis-assemble and reassemble, mostly mechanical things. Always a challenge, and I developed very good eye-hand dexterity that I still enjoy. Then, and until very recently, I did not realize my learning struggles were any different from those experienced by anyone else. Consequently, I didn't think that I was different so far as learning is concerned.

EARLY WORKPLACE EXPERIENCE

[1957–1990] Some types of work are ideally suited to the dyslexic worker. Fortunately, the types of work I chose were ideally suited to my personal learning style.

1. Electronics and Ground Communication in the Royal Canadian Air Force
2. Computer Hardware Assembly and Programming at IBM
3. Computer Technical Support and Programming in industry
4. Computer Technical Support and Programming Management in various industries

In all of these positions, my visual learning abilities afforded me a level of growth and success I would not otherwise have achieved.

DISCOVERY

One of the most difficult things I've had to face was the recent dis-covery [fall, 1991] that I have a learning disability. In a first-year uni-versity psychology project, students were required to analyze their per-sonal study habits. In my report, I described in some detail a difficulty I encountered during the study. To me, the problem was normal but the person reviewing the study thought otherwise. As a result, I was invited to participate in Sue Weaver's doctoral thesis research project (part of her studies at the University of Toronto).

Further analysis was also conducted by The Learning Loft and the Ivy Clinical Audiology Centre. To make a long story short, there were clin-ical reasons for the difficulties I was experiencing, and, no, the problem would not go away. Coming to grips with this learning disability and accepting that there is a real limitation in my ability to achieve academ-ically has been, and, to some extent, still is, very difficult. It was not until this time that I discovered my parents knew, from a very early age, that I had learning disabilities.

Accepting this limitation, or any other limitation for that matter, is not something I do well. Therefore, like any other problem I had run into, I had a new challenge.

Where to start? Because a major component of most of my jobs had been staff development and training, I had developed many techniques to help others apply their basic knowledge to problem solving. Using this building block approach was also very effective in developing staff strengths and knowledge. When I applied these techniques to myself, I was able to work my way out of the swamp, so to speak, and clearly demonstrated to myself that I had workable options.

INHIBITORS

So, I had to work out how to constructively deal with things that negatively affected my progress. These are detailed in what follows.

1. FRUSTRATION AND NEGATIVE FEELINGS

I find the worst thing about frustration is that it tends to sneak up on me, displacing the original problem and becoming my focal point. This, in turn fosters tension and negative feelings about my ability to accomplish whatever I was doing. Working together, frustration and negative feelings are very destructive and can be very difficult to deal with.

2. COMMON SCHOOL PROBLEMS

These problems were ever-present companions throughout all my formal education and were particularly troublesome during my forays into post-secondary education. At college and university, I experienced a large helping of overload when I carried too many courses. It seemed that the harder I tried, the worse the results. The result was that all subjects suffered, and I became very frustrated. For me, this was a recipe for failure. The only practical solution was to reduce my course load. Once done, I was able to catch up and work successfully. But reducing the course load also increased the cost and time required to graduate.

3 DISTRACTIONS AND UNCONTROLLED FOCUS

Distraction and uncontrolled focus come in many flavours. For example, because I must be consciously aware of the world around me, my focus will occasionally shift from a class presentation, and I'll lose the continuity of the presentation. Also, while taking notes, my focus shifts from the presentation to writing, and I miss what's being said or parts of what is being said randomly creep into the notes. Trying to use these notes often consumes a great deal of time and can result in more confusion and frustration.

Fortunately, when studying, I can effectively turn off the outside world. But when you want to get my attention, you often have to touch me to queue me back to the outside world again. This still drives my family to distraction, pun intended.

4. Theory-Based versus Knowledge-Based Teaching

Perhaps the most difficult learning problem I've had to deal with is the presentation sequence of new material. Theory-Based Teaching—teaching with an increasing number of small unrelated—details makes—it very difficult for me to learn. However, Knowledge-Based Teaching—Teaching that begins with a defined construct then builds down to—detail makes—it much easier for me to learn. Although I fully appreciate that some people may initially prefer theory-based learning, I have found from personal experience teaching in a technical environment, that the structure of knowledge-based teaching has always worked better for everyone because it always exposes the how and why as learning progresses.

5 How Dyslexia Affects My Everyday Life and the Way I Learn.

1. Reading can be difficult; therefore, it needs to be practised regularly. I find that if I don't read regularly for a few weeks, my reading rate will fall to about 25% of my normal. Therefore, if possible, I read every day.

2. When I'm reading, if a word is misinterpreted, the error may not be recognized. Later in the text when the error becomes apparent, I must go back over the text to re-establish proper context and meaning. This type of word substitution can be very common and is not always easy to detect.

3. Another common problem is locating my place on the page when I look up from what I'm reading. Very often, I must scan around the page to locate my place in the text. This also makes copying from the board or another text very difficult and time consuming.

4. Building on an existing knowledge base is always easier and therefore more successful. Even with new material, there are often parallels and links to existing knowledge that can help me master the new material.

5. For me, it is very clear that interesting subjects are easier to learn. What is not so obvious is that too much new material, even interesting material, can result in information overload.

6. If something doesn't work the first time, I don't give up. The adage, if at first you don't succeed then try again, has been and still is a very real part of my life.

7. I do not allow myself to be limited by the knowledge that I have a learning disability. Achievement has been and, to some extent, still is a very real struggle.

8. I am developing an awareness of my limitations. For example, if I take on too much at once, I find that even simple tasks are difficult. This can be VERY BAD because the frustration becomes a focal point and blocks the very things I am trying to achieve.

9. When writing, spelling can be a problem if I don't pay close attention to what I'm doing. But, like reading, it improves with practice. I am in constant competition with my spell checker to catch my spelling errors before it does. This little game has helped me improve my spelling.

NEXT STEPS

THE POSITIVE SIDE OF DYSLEXIA

After two abortive attempts at higher education, I found a way through my personal learning difficulties using methods developed by Ronald D. Davis at the Reading Research Council in California. Following training in the Davis Methods, I then began working with children and adults that were saddled with similar so-called learning disabilities. Using the strengths of dyslexia can turn learning disabilities into learning abilities.

A CLOSER LOOK AT THE PROBLEM

It is important to remember that as dyslexics we have a lower-than-normal threshold of confusion. This is especially prevalent when we are confronted with an unfamiliar situation, time pressure, or a change in our environment. A disorientation can also be triggered very suddenly when we look at letters, words, symbols, numbers, or anything else we don't recognize or understand. For example, when reading we may recognize a word this time we see it, but the next time we see it—be it on the same line, paragraph, page, etc.—it may appear to us as a completely new and mysterious word. If we are reading aloud, the word you hear may bear no resemblance to the word printed on the page. However, the word you hear is the word we believe we see.

The common in-school remedy is drill, but unfortunately these only cause confusion and disorientation and makes learning even more difficult. Very counterproductive.

Because we are holistic, multidimensional thinkers, with a low tolerance for confusion, it can be difficult for us:

1. To work with letters, symbols, words, math, and different fonts
2. To cope with hand and body kinesthetics that result in loss of balance and coordination
3. To participate in team sports and activities
4. To understand spoken and written words

But, when we use tools and methods suited to our unique learning style, we can learn to read, write, spell, listen, do math, and study efficiently. Then we are able to build upon our creative and imaginative strengths and work and play more productively without peers.

Help for Dyslexic Children and Adults

When a learning disability has its roots in confusion-triggered disorientation then there is much that can be done to turn the disability into an ability.

Steps to Overcome Disorientation

Because confusion triggered disorientation is a common factor in many learning situations it is important to identify and resolve personal disorientation triggers. Procedures identified in the following steps will help identify and resolve common sources of confusion-triggered disorientation.

Begin by resolving balance and coordination difficulties:

1. Learn how to recognize and control disorientation.
2. Learn how to improve balance and eye-hand coordination.
3. Learn how to improve auditory disorientation.

Identify and resolve basic language-triggered disorientation:

1. Letter-triggered disorientation—learning the alphabet is NOT a song.
2. Trigger word disorientation—all the small words that have no natural picture associated with them (the dolche list sight words and others).

Identify and resolve common symbol sourced disorientation:

1. Learn to recognize and understand common symbols as found in signs, directions, etc.

2. Learn to resolve spacial relationship terms—front, back, ahead, behind, besides, between, etc.

3. Learn to resolve numeral confusions—quantity, size, bigger-than smaller-than etc.

4. Resolve simple math functions and symbols—add, subtract, multiply, and divide.

5. Look at how various fonts can distort meaning recognize how various common fonts change letter form.

As well as the basics noted above, there are a number of life concepts that also need to be mastered. These concept words form an essential foundation for life and learning.

1. Self—a sense of who we are and how the general parts of self interact with the other (the world around us). When you have a clear understanding of self then self, can be easily included in all the following words.

2. Change—how something becomes something else, including the concepts of before, after, cause, and effect.

3. Consequence—every action, no matter how small, has a consequence, and consequences come in positive and negative forms. Although consequence is often associated with discipline, this is a very small part of the full scope of consequence. It is very important to emphasize the positive aspect of consequence.

4. Standard—something that does not change, e.g. ruler markings, the numbers on a clock face, and others.

5. Time—although there are many aspects of time, they all relate in one way or another to seconds, minutes, hours, days, weeks, years, seasons, age, etc. The standard of time is the rotation of the earth on its axis and the orbit of the earth around the sun.

6. Sequence—the concept of sequence is fundamental to counting and the ability to count is fundamental to all mathematics. Sequence is also fundamental to the way things happen in everyday life. Everything exists or happens in one or more sequences. Sequence includes the concepts of size, amount, order, time, and importance.

7. Order Versus Disorder—has to do with the way things are in the world around us and includes the concepts of place, position, or condition. Whether something is in order or in disorder may depend on the observer.

8. Choose and Choice—when you choose you decide which thing or person you want out of the ones that are available. Choice is what happens as a consequence of what you choose.

In closing, when you help others, always remember that you are working with an ability and always strive to provide achievable challenges that build self-confidence, self-assurance, and success. And keep in mind that everyone sees with their own eyes, feels with their own emotions, and learns at their own pace. Be patient.

Always keep in mind that our natural ability and preference is to think holistically; therefore, we are not naturally constrained by any thinking boundaries. We are often asked if we think outside the box. Box? What box?

Learning to Love Myself
By Brianna Longhenry

I'm not like the typical person who has autism. My doctors use to refer me as a person that has "notebook" autism, meaning that my behaviours, when written down, described what you would find in any definition of what autism is with regards to having problems with audio and visual stimuli and repetitive behaviours. However, when you meet me in person, I am sociable. I make eye contact. I'm shy at first, but I do put the effort in to communicate with others. They would then be surprised at my diagnosis.

Yet in grade eight, my family doctor basically told my parents not to send me to high school and to instead work on teaching me basic life skills. The doctor said that with my education level, I would not succeed in life and basically told my parents how I could get financial help (welfare or disability). I remember driving home that day in the back seat of the car and saying to my mom, "Am I really a failure? Is he right that I won't go anywhere in life?"

My mom, my biggest supporter, laughed and said, "Brianna, together we are going to show them how wrong they are, you can do absolutely anything you want in life." That day, I started self-teaching. I'd go onto Google and join homeschool class groups, I self-taught reading and math. I was determined not to be labeled as unfixable.

I did graduate high school with an IEP and lots of work and I remember a week after getting my diploma sending a quick email to that doctor who straight out told my parents not to waste years on high school but to just teach me life skills.

As an adult, the sights, sounds, and smells of everyday existence still overwhelm me. I struggle with everything from waking up to staying on task, which is important, as when I was twenty, I had a baby. I now have a toddler I'm responsible for. I quickly get exhausted in other people's company as I'm mentally trying to keep up with conversations and stay engaged. I'm trying to hear and process what they're saying, watch body language and tone of voice, mimic their facial expressions, and most of all I'm trying to be "normal." My brain has to go through so many steps consciously that other people don't even think about. I feel like everyone is on a smooth road, and I'm driving through a deep wooded trail.

I have completely accepted my autism, and I hope that I can be someone who can make others who have autism realize that they DON'T need to be defined as the person with autism and that they can feel important and accepted and not thrown in the back of a classroom like I was. I want nothing more than to teach others to self-advocate and to teach people what autism really is.

I don't want other kids to have to go through what I did. I want our society to be more accepting and knowledgeable of what autism is, and the only way to do that is by listening to autistic people. I have recently been able to speak my truth about myself more openly on social media. Being online is almost like a protection, as they can't see me. I'm protected behind a keyboard and online identity.

It is so important to find safety and security talking to others and not holding the self-hate in, as for many years I hated everything about me. I couldn't understand why others looked so happy and could slide through life without the issues I face every day.

Trying too hard to fit in or to even be understood has caused me so much anxiety and depression. As I have become older, I have accepted me for who I am. I will never allow autism to define me, ever!! I, Brianna Longhenry, define me, not anyone's views on autism. I own my autism; it does not own me.

I guess I will end this by simply saying, self-love and self-advocating are key for every person, especially for those on the spectrum because we can so easily get swept away and unnoticed.

RECIPE—SOFT RICOTTA CHEESE COOKIES (MY COMFORT FOOD) BY BRIANNA LONGHENRY

INGREDIENTS

2 cups white sugar
1 cup of softened butter
I tub (15 0z) ricotta cheese
2 large eggs
3/4 cups of chocolate chips
2 tsp of vanilla
4 cups of sugar
2 tbsp of baking powder
1 tsp of salt

Step 1: Preheat oven to 350° F
Step 2: Beat together sugar and butter in a large bowl with an electric mixer on low speed until combined. Increase speed to high and beat until light and fluffy, about 5 minutes.

Step 3: Reduce speed to medium and beat in ricotta, eggs, and vanilla, slowly add chocolate chips

Step 4: Drop level tablespoonfuls of dough 2 inches apart onto the prepared baking sheets.

Step 5: Bake in the preheated oven until cookies are very lightly golden and soft, about 15 minutes. Use a spatula to remove cookies to a wire rack to cool completely.

Nightmare Level Unlocked: Living with Multiple Disabilities
By Corey Kearns

I was born with two physical birth defects which have complicated and still are complicating my life in various ways. The first birth defect I was born with was undeveloped retinas which caused me to be born legally blind. I had to wear glasses 24/7 before the age of two because without them everything was blurry shapes. The second birth defect is a club foot, for which I required surgery because my foot was curled up in a ball. I got a really cool looking feather scar from the surgery, and it extends from the side of my foot to above my ankle. I am currently classified as half blind, and I have no far sight capabilities in my eyes anymore, even with my glasses.

I learned to control what my eyes focus on because if I don't, my vision blurs and I get headaches. This means I can be staring out of my window, and I will only see a specific detail of a specific car, and, from there, I will move my focus from object to object until I find what I'm looking for. This trick allows me to spot darker shades of the same colours inside those colours. It helps me spot my black furred dog in the middle of night when he's moving around.

I still struggle with visual issues like telling the difference between colours that are too similar especially when it comes to opacity. I can't rely on colour coding because of this or any other kind of colour system. I have difficulties cooking because I can't tell if things are cooked based on my vision. I have to sit inches from my tv or computer monitor to be able to see anything, and, unfortunately, the size of the tv or monitor doesn't matter anymore due to the lack of far sight capabilities in my eyes.

My feet aren't doing so great either. In fact, at the time of writing this, my feet have been consistently swollen for months. I have been dealing with foot pain on and off since I was little, so I've learned tricks like shifting my feet so I'm walking on a specific part of my foot to reduce pain. I learned how to stand so that my weight spreads out in a way that makes it manageable. I do, however, struggle with balance. I suffer from chronic pain, and it gets bad quickly whenever I have to walk or stand on uneven surfaces. This is because I have absolutely no arch in either of my feet.

I was diagnosed with autism and Schizoid-Affective Disorder: Bipolar Type when I was eight. I suffer from hallucinations, obsessive paranoia, frequent bouts of crippling depression, I get overwhelmed easily, and I struggle with some social cues. I was also diagnosed with ADHD and C-PTSD (Complex Post Traumatic Syndrome Disorder) at different points in my life. I have way more trauma triggers than even I can keep track of at times, and I either struggle to focus on anything, or I focus so completely on one thing that it becomes the only thing in existence.

The ADHD can make things difficult because it's not your typical lack of focus, it's like activities or tasks run away from your brain the more you try to focus on them. It can cause my vision to blur and my thoughts to vanish and it's rough. Then there's hyperfocus which is when you get so sucked into a task that the entire world is just gone, there's no other sounds and no other sights. In this state, my focus is so completely centered on the task that I lose track of everything else. I will forget to eat, sleep, shower, and everything else, too. In this state of mind, 12 hours can feel like one hour, and, until my brain breaks away from the activity, I would never know.

C-PTSD can complicate things on multiple levels because it's caused by more than one traumatic event reinforcing the same trigger or several different events causing multiple triggers.

Schizoid-Affective Disorder: Bipolar Type is a particularly nasty disability that combines the manic highs and lows of bipolar disorder with the symptoms of paranoid schizophrenia. But it also includes major depressive disorder. Imagine suffering from frequent and random periods of depression that are made worse by the bipolar side of this disability. Then, during these periods, you suffer from obsessively paranoid thoughts that can be caused by the smallest thing like a raised tone or a shift in facial expressions. Then, the trauma triggers kick in and suddenly you're frozen in place, stunned by the thoughts and brutal memories that start circling your mind. This spiraling combination of symptoms drains your energy, your focus, your motivation, and can lead to an emotionally hollow feeling that feels like your entire self is being sucked into a black hole centered at your gut.

So far, I've learned to cope with these things by adopting and building up a neutral mentality and training my brain to skip straight to acceptance. This allows me to process any paranoid thoughts by thinking, "If it's true, I can't do anything about it so I can't stress." I make sure I have an arsenal of distractions to help center myself when I become overwhelmed. I learned to meditate on the move so that even when I'm overwhelmed or stressed, I can center my mental state whenever and wherever. I can't think of all my coping tricks off the top of my head, but I've developed, honed, and continue to refine each of them.

All of my disabilities have seriously impacted my life in a variety of ways. I am afraid of almost everything, so, to overcome that, I had to learn to run headfirst into most things to avoid allowing the fear to settle in. I struggle with sense of self, emotional understanding, social cues, and everyday things. Things such as cooking, cleaning, hygiene, watching tv, reading, and a lot more. A part of me is always preparing to isolate and even tries to pull me back into the recluse I worked so hard to stop being. I can be okay one day and struggling to eat, sleep, and focus the next because of crippling depression. I have to push myself every second just to not disappear, because every fiber of my being is trying to pull me into isolation. I have to tune out or sit with a hundred different paranoid thoughts triggered by the smallest things.

One part of my brain is constantly trying to convince me that my friends and family will turn on me for saying the wrong thing, let alone any bigger mistakes. The other tries to remind me I won't know until it happens, so it's not helping to stress over it. Then, there's the social situations, you see. When I'm depressed, the hyper-vigilance I developed from my childhood trauma is twice as sensitive. I feel every look, I notice every shift in a person's stance, and I even hear the smallest shift in tone too. Unfortunately, when I'm in this state my brain interprets every one of these social cues as me having done something wrong. The problem is, no matter how many times I try to rework my thoughts, my brain obsessively backtracks to the same thoughts and refuses to let go.

Living alone on the spectrum is hard enough, but living on the spectrum with mental illnesses and physical disabilities is a nightmare.

Creamy Mushrooms with Noodles
By Corey Kearns

Ingredients

- A can of cream of mushroom soup
- Pasta (the type doesn't matter)
- Butter or milk (optional, it depends on how you like your noodles)

Kitchenware Needed

- A cooking pot (a bowl can be used if you don't have access to a stove).
- A stove (you can use a kettle, microwave or even a campfire anything that lets you boil the water will do).
- A strainer (you can place a plate or cover over the pot to drain noodles to just be careful the water will be hot).

Cooking Instructions

- Boil water
- Place noodles in water
- Cook noodles
- Drain noodles
- Optional: Add milk or butter to noodles

Fun tip: A small bit of water can be used instead of milk it just won't be as creamy

1. Open can of cream of mushroom soup.
2. Pour can in pot with noodles.
3. Stir cream of mushroom in with the noodles.
4. Enjoy.

Perseverance & Accommodations Got Me Here!
By Elliot Smith

Independence means that I can show others that I can do strong and very hard things on my own. Independence also means that I can push myself to continue to do hard work, too. It means I can do things without the support of others, even if I have had support to begin with that taught me how to do these tasks independently.

Being independent is important to me because it means I can do things on my own, even when my mom or grandparents are not around to help me. If I am taught the right way and with support, I can learn how to do things independently. It may take me longer, and I may learn differently from others, but I can get there. It shows I can be strong and persevere even when others may think I can't do it.

There are a lot of new things that I have been taught properly how to do on my own. I can shop for groceries for my mom as a favour and help out as a chore. I can spend money wisely by using my debit or credit card for smaller or larger purchases, whether they are needs or wants. I can take the bus to the Abilities Centre on my own independently for personal training or if I have to get to work, because my mom can't drive me all the time. I actually had a worker who taught me how to take the GO Train on my own all the way downtown, as I worked at the Rogers Centre one summer. This worker would ride the train with me to show me at first. She then stopped taking the train to see if I could do it on my own and met me downtown. I was able to follow the instructions perfectly as she wrote them down for me on my phone. I also had apps on my phone that I could check that helped me with the GO Train times. I did the same thing to learn how to take the bus on my own to my present job and also use a special app to help with the bus times. Being able to do these things on my own makes me feel very confident.

Currently, I work at the Abilities Centre as a Physical Fitness and Literacy Associate and Mixed Ability Sport Facilitator. It took a long time for me to get here though. I went to different job programs in the community to learn how to interview, how to do my resume and how to keep a job. I found a job coach who works with adults with autism, and he taught me how to do a good interview. Once I got the job, my job coach came with me to my job every day to make sure I was being taught the way I needed to be taught so I could learn what tasks I had to do when I was working. My job coach slowly started coming less and less so I could do the job more and more on my own. He helped teach me how to self-advocate and get things into place, such as accommodations.

One of the accommodations I had were to get a task list with times on it so I could check off what I was to do every half hour. I also learned how to put alarms in my phone to help me move from one task to the next. My employer lets me listen to music too when I am needing to relax, but I can only use one bud in one ear in case a customer has to ask me a question, so it is for safety purposes. My job coach stopped coming because I had shown I could stand on my own two feet. I realized then that I have a lot of independence under my belt!

I have come a long way, and you can too with the right support and right teacher. I am hoping I can next learn how to cook on my own, but that will be the next thing to look forward to. It is good to have goals. I am hoping that my support worker will help to teach me how to do some easy things so I can make a simple meal. It is important to be independent so you can show others that you can do it, that the sky is the limit, and nothing is impossible.

Eating, Exercise and Energy

Mom's Musings:

Elliot, like many of us, has had to work on keeping a close eye on his weight and lifestyle. He is on medication that is necessary to help him regulate better and manage his ADHD symptoms. Medication, in conjunction with learning about healthy lifestyle and using regulation strategies, is what has made Elliot successful. However, the side effects are such that medication causes weight gain, so we are continuously monitoring controlling weight with healthy meal choices, as well as lots of sports and activities to keep him as fit as we can. Elliot's love of sports is what got him into this area, and it has been wonderful watching him create a budding career in the area of health and wellness.

Elliot's POV:

I do personal training with my personal trainer in order to help relieve my anxiety. I also walk to help manage my fitness log, as well as my steps.

The sports that I am involved with are baseball at Durham Region Challenger Baseball, footbal at Pickering Football Club Advanced All Abilities League, rugby at Mixed Ability Rugby at Oshawa Vikings Rugby Club, and my ASD Archery League at Archery 2. I have done these activities to stay fit and to help manage my weight, plus I enjoy making lots of new friends. Sports keep me active for a reason, they make me feel good about myself. Sports help me manage my anxiety and help me work up a sweat when I am feeling overstimulated. Sports are there to help me work with good coaches and make me work with amazing athletes. Finally, I think that these four sports help me keep active because:

- In baseball, I hit for power and move defensively and offensively,

- In soccer I run and kick for the ball when I go on defense and offense,

- In rugby I tackle for the rugby ball and score tries in rugby to get hat tricks.

- In archery, I have to aim for the bullseye and work as a team player in my archery league with all my friends who are on the spectrum of ASD.

Therefore, these results all show I have to persevere and be a strong athlete since I am fit enough to work hard as an athlete in any sport.

I have learned from a lot of my past employers and coaches about healthy eating. When I was younger, I thought that I was never going to lose weight, but then I showed people wrong and started walking an hour every day and have lost some weight now. By the time I was in my late teen years, I started to eat more fruit and vegetables and started to drink more bottled and carbonated water.

I also got into yoga and meditation as well. Yoga helps me de-stress my anxiety and makes me feel more relaxed. Meditation makes me think about positive thoughts and lets me have a positive bright future ahead of me. Finally, I think that I am going to go places if I eat healthy because the more I stay away from bad foods, the more I will succeed and moderate in order to train for more marathons.

Sports and fitness are so important to me because I learned that it is never too early to start when playing sports or working out. The reason why I am involved with baseball, soccer, rugby, and archery is because these sports help me build self-confidence by making sure that I am playing as a team with my teammates and working together, leaving no man behind. Fitness helps me train for sports. The reason why fitness helps me is because I train for marathons by eating healthy (fruits and vegetables) and drinking bottled water and Perrier. I also train for sports by making sure that I feel less stressed by being more awake and self-regulated.

Fitness also helps me deal with stress because after a nice long one to two-hour workout, I usually feel better and stay hydrated. I usually train on the field house track at the Abilities Centre and usually do four or five laps around the track. Then, I do the fitness bicycle, and then I end up doing the treadmill and the cross trainer. I also like to lift dumbbells and do pectoral flys, as well as rear deltoids, squat thrusts, and, finally, last but not least, push up, pull down.

Later, by the time my workout is halfway done, I usually go into the weight room and go into doing machines like back extension, body extension, biceps and triceps, abdomen, pec deck, optimal rhomb, etc.

However, I even have gotten into yoga too. Yoga helps me manage my anxiety and makes me feel more relaxed and calmer. Yoga is a strategy that I use to help do stretches and warmups to show that I feel healthy and good after I usually do a one-hour session of yoga. Furthermore, meditation helps me as well, meditation makes me feel calm and makes me not listen to negative thoughts and makes them turn into positive thoughts.

I am always known to use my Calm App on my phone to help calm myself down when I am hearing negative voices inside my head. Negativity doesn't solve the problem. Both yoga and meditation help me manage my anxiety and ASD because I know that both of these strategy tools make me feel great and positive when I am feeling down. Having a good positive life is important because the more you exercise, the less likely you will gain any weight. After all, I work hard so that I can live a long healthy, happy life!

I have had a lot of involvement with the Abilities Centre over the years and a great opportunity presented itself in this area. Not only did I get hired as a Physical Fitness and Literacy Associate, I also was asked to join the Mixed Abilities Sports Inclusion Team. This team meets once a week and talks about how to get the Mixed Ability Sport model out to all sports leagues. Mixed Ability Sport is a way of doing sport where all abilities participate on the same team so there are no barriers, and it is full inclusion. I now help train coaches by talking about my personal experience as an athlete with a disability. The first thing I did was to earn my Mixed Abilities Coaching Certificate, because I am a good leader for coaching teams and being a good sports ambassador for any community team around Durham Region. I also participated on the Sports Inclusion Team by giving many suggestions to make sports better like having 3-min warnings to signal a transition to a break or change in game or to have pictures to show different sport moves as some players are visual learners.

The first team I joined with the Mixed Ability Rugby League was the Oshawa Vikings Club. I first learned how to play flag rugby, but we were invited to be the first team to represent Canada at the IMAS International Mixed Ability Sport Tournament. We played against 24 other teams from all around the world in Ireland (Cork). We actually came in second so we were World Cup Finalists! The women's team, the Trailbrazers, came in third and got a bronze cup. I actually scored my first try and got to shoot the boot! Shooting the boot is a rugby tradition where you have to drink (in my case it was a pop) out of a teammate's dirty rugby boot! I met so many people from all around the world. Everyone was treated the same, and I have never in my life felt more a part of a team and something huge in my whole entire life. This tournament showed that we can all get along and that we can all be treated the same and play the same sport.

I also play other sports that are not Mixed Ability (but maybe one day they will be!), such as soccer. I am on the Learn to Train team and will start volunteering for the All Abilities teams in the Fall. My leagues have badges that you can earn when working on special projects outside the team. So far, I have earned the Fitness Badge, the Volunteering Badge, The Discovery Badge, the Coaching Badge and the Disability Awareness Badge. I earned the disability awareness badge for showing awareness towards other disabilities. These badges all required tasks to be completed in order to earn the actual badge and some of them took several months to complete. One badge I am very proud of was the Volunteering Badge where I organized a walking fundraiser for my league and raised $2,500 dollars and walked over 6 hours to complete it. All of these badges and opportunities have made me a better athlete by helping to build on my leadership skills.

All of these opportunities, IMART, Soccer Badges Program, the Sports Inclusion Team, have helped me land my dream job. The dream job that I got was the Physical Fitness and Literacy Associate at the Abilities Centre in Whitby. I got this job for a reason. I got this job because I had to show proof that I was the most improved athlete in all of Durham Region despite not making any rep sports teams in high school or outside of school. I only made the cut to play on recreational sports teams in Durham Region. I also got this job because I work hard and had been doing many co-op placements throughout high school as well as volunteering at the Abilities Centre. Volunteering really does go a long way, so I always say it is worth starting out this way to get your foot in the door. I have been working at the Abilities Centre since about 2021 when the pandemic started. I recently was asked to help teach Rugby with a coworker to the Thrive Camp participants, and it was a huge success!

Mom's Musings:

Elliot continues to surpass all our expectations. Every year, he does something new or different that makes us realise there are no limits for him. Not only did he graduate college, but he is also now working part time at a fitness centre. He participated in representing Canada at the IMART tournament, something we never thought possible. I never dreamed in a million years I would see him compete on a world stage with athletes of all abilities, especially after years of being told "he can't," we have now shown the world "he can." Most importantly, this Mixed Ability Rugby team has shown there are no barriers. Several of the players have gone on to do bigger and better things with their lives as well. One player helps to volunteer with the younger rugby leagues, another is now playing in the U2 men's league, a third is working for one of the players at a pizza truck, and the fourth is sitting on the Board of Directors for the Vikings Club (that is Elliot, of course). The benefits of having this type of league show inclusion reaches not just the sport but beyond.

Graduating College: Situations, Struggles, and Success

Mom's Musings:

I never thought college was going to be possible. I kept hearing that voice in my head from a teacher who said he would never get there. After the hard years, things seemed to settle down and we got into a real rhythm. Elliot was determined to get to college. He had a goal, and he wanted very badly to get there. We found Community Integration through Co-operative Education, a program we saw was a perfect fit. Only some colleges have this program as it is a very specific program designed to help students with intellectual or physical disabilities. Elliot applied to five colleges that all had the CICE program. Each one had a required interview as part of the component to gain entry. Elliot surpassed all expectations and managed to get into all the programs, with the exception of where he got waitlisted at one of them. We finally decided on Fleming after a lot of thought as we liked the small town feel there, liked the balance between academic and life skills courses, and thought that if he was not near home, he would have the opportunity to live in residence.

I was convinced I would have to move to another city where the college was, as I could not envision my son being able to navigate a new city, new people. He had never been away from me for one night on his own. I had heart palpitations thinking of him living on his own. He had never been away from me or our family, how would he manage to live on his own? I can recall thinking I needed to start looking at apartments, but the head of the CICE program we were interested in told me I needed to let him try residence. She said if he did not do well at that point, I could consider moving up here with him. I held my breath and didn't breathe or sleep for months.

ELLIOT'S INSIGHTS:

The biggest challenge for me while away at college was dealing with homesickness. I cried in class sometimes to help me feel better when dealing with homesickness. Some days were harder than others. It was my first time ever away from home and my family, so that was a real struggle for me.

A lot of the students in our program were still living at home, so they could not understand why or how hard it really was for me. I also had difficulties with understanding peers' perspectives. There were a few kids that looked at my homesickness as a weakness because they believed there was no crying in class if you were a college student. They thought that I should not be crying and should instead act like a man. I thought the way they treated me was rude and disrespectful because they said to me that there was no crying in class because it was college. I got upset and stormed out of the classroom. I took breaks in the quiet room and sometimes raised my voice when getting frustrated with people I didn't get along well with.

Over time, and with the help from my IFs (instructional facilitators similar to EAs), I was able to better handle these situations. My IFs let me go to the quiet room where I could call my mom and talk it through with her. They also let me take laps and listen to music as this was a very good strategy for me when dealing with these situations.

Another challenge I faced was living on my own for the very first time in my life. I would stay up at residence Monday to Thursday and then would come home on Thursday night and have a long weekend as we did not have classes on Friday. Coming home every weekend was also another way I could learn to overcome my homesickness.

I had to get used to being independent up at residence as well. I had to learn how to heat up my meals my mom would send up, how to clean my room and make my bed every day. I had to get myself ready for class and follow a very complicated schedule. Do you know I was never late for one class? I even learned how to lock my door every day. These things may seem simple, but they were huge things I had to learn for the very first time at the age of 19. So, I had to learn not only how to manage my college and class schedule, but I also had to learn how to live independently on top of that. The biggest thing I learned was to do my homework on my own up at residence in between classes. I worked so hard during the week, so I had to bring very little home on the weekends. Again, this is important because it meant when I came home every weekend, I could really use the time to relax and feel good about myself. Remember my earlier chapter? Schoolwork is for school and home is for relaxing.

There were times in my first year I was really sad because getting used to grown up life was tough for me. I cried for help because homesickness makes us all feel down. The first year was tough. Independence was not easy the first year in college.

I was doing really well in residence because I made my bed by myself and showed up to class on time. I even made food from home in my residence microwave. In my second year, my roommates and I won the cleanest suite award! Now that is an accomplishment. During the two years I was at residence, I was well supported by support workers from Community Living Trent Highlands. Sometimes they just needed to give me a push when dealing with my difficulties, in residence such as homesickness and being with all new people in a new city. However, Community Living is there for help because they taught me the life skills in order to help with looking after myself independently.

Furthermore, my support workers took me on outings in the community to help me deal with stress and not be so isolated. I would go to the movies, swimming, and, sometimes, we even went to bowl. My workers also helped me to learn how to take the bus to my co-op placements on my own. They would practice taking the route with me, and then they sent me on my own to see if I could do it. Well guess what? I did it with no issues. I took the bus to my different placements, which were at a thrift store and at the local OHL hockey rink.

I think the important lesson here is learning that even if you are living in a new city not knowing anyone, you can still be successful and learn how to take a new transit system to get around. Most people might think that this is not a big deal, but for someone with autism and all the changes and new places, it was huge—and I did it!

There were times my Community Living workers helped me learn how to deal with anxiety, fears, and how to defuse conflict with peers in my classroom. They would just spend time with me talking through all these social situations and give me tips on how to better manage them. I would not be where I am today without the support of them.

Despite all the challenges, I was still able to graduate with my diploma from the CICE program. I was on the honour roll for all four semesters too. Upon graduating, I learned that I was receiving the Ellen Murphy award for most improved student. It was nice to know that others saw how hard I worked trying to manage all the changes, the new city, the new places and new people. So many changes make me feel very overwhelmed which is why I had a hard time first year fitting in. My IF told me, "Elliot, you are a strong person who can do hard things." So, this quote became my quote for the whole two years I was at college.

I was a part of a few groups at college. I was involved with the Student Beat and would do live radio shows at college telling people about some of the social programs and events there. I was also involved with the Halloween Fundraiser where we carved pumpkins and delivered them to people who showed up to our fundraiser. I even did my TSN radio play-by-play fundraiser where I impersonated Jack Armstrong of TSN Raptors Basketball during a Special Olympics vs CICE students' game.

As mentioned, the CICE program held fundraisers in the college a few times a year. We invited Cody Crowley to talk at the college. He is the undefeated UFC Lightweight Champion born and raised in Peterborough, Ontario, Canada, and he helps to train Floyd Mayweather now in Vegas, USA. Cody Crowley came over to do a public talk on mental health and having a healthy lifestyle, he talked about enjoying a healthy life and how to look after your body and your mind. Do you know the funny thing? One day my support worker saw I had a picture of Cody Crowley in my room, and he said, "Hey, did you know that is my cousin?" What a small world. Cody taught me it doesn't matter how hard you fall—it is about how you get back up!

We also held an event for Austin Riley and his autism experience through racing. Austin Riley is the first ever openly autistic race car driver. He even talked about where his passion for racing came from and how it all started. I learned that his saying is, "I raise awareness for autism, one lap at a time." Austin Riley taught me that you do not have to be a superstar at racing, but that you need to do what makes you happy. Austin is a very successful racer and has won the Nissan Micra Cup Championship Race three times back-to-back in 2014, 2017, and 2018.

Austin Riley is a part of a racing foundation called Racing with Autism, which is a foundation that helps kids who are on the spectrum with ASD.

Austin and Cody were very inspirational to me while I was studying at college. I thought if they could do it, so could I. I also had several teachers and IFs that were inspirational to me and helped me get to where I am. My most inspirational teacher helped me learn about having a healthy lifestyle, being independent, and learning how to work as a team in the CICE program. I also had my most inspirational IF who helped me learn how to deal with anxiety and triggers. She even helped me learn how to feel less stressed by listening to music as a stress reliever. She helped me with my mantra for the two years I was at Fleming College: "I am a strong person who can do very hard things."

My IF also helped with all of my accommodations including having extra time when completing exams. She helped me stay focused and made sure I was always on top of my work. Finally, it was also great seeing her because she always put a smile on my face when she always asked me, "What great things have you done today?"

MOM'S MUSINGS:

The only reason why college and living on residence was a success was due to the creation of yet another village. I had enlisted the help of two Community Living Support Workers who went in a few hours a night to help Elliot with basic life skills. They would also take him out in the community to do fun things like movies or swimming. The program at college was also well supported. There was one IF to every four or five students. These IFs had a similar role to an EA. They helped to make accommodations for the students and were a lifeline to all the kids in this program. Elliot was fortunate to have some great IFs and teachers that were patient, forgiving, and who kept pushing him to be the best that he could be.

We have always tried to replicate this village wherever we go now. Our kids and loved ones on the spectrum will truly only be successful if they have the support built around them so they feel included and valued as a true part of their community. It is true—it takes a village to raise a child. We have been fortunate enough to always build a strong and supportive village everywhere Elliot goes, and that's why he thrives. All of our children are different and need different things, but if there is one small piece of advice, I have for you, it would be to build your villages. This is the key to your child's success.

INDEPENDENCE, INITIATIVE AND INSPIRING

MOM'S MUSINGS:

Transitioning into Adulthood has been the hardest part, because, once your child reaches a particular age, they are discharged or released from services. It truly does feel like falling off a cliff with no one there to catch you. There is so little out there for our kids once they become adults. Most parents do the usual applying for financial supports like DSO and ODSP (Ontario Disability Support Program), but, beyond that, finding programming can sometimes be like a needle in a haystack. We have been fortunate through all our community connections to find those places, and I cannot say enough about Grandview Children's Centre and the Abilities Centre who have stepped up and seen my son's worth.

Besides sitting on committees at both of these places and being a contributing member, he now, as mentioned, works for one of them. Any parent would agree all we want is for them to feel like they are valued, contributing members of society as they have so much to give, and we have so much to learn from them.

ELLIOT'S POV:

I have gained independence for a reason so that I can show others I am able to do things on my own. I gained independence because that is how I learned how to make my own meals from scratch in residence at Fleming College. I had support workers from Community Living who came into my residence in the evening to help show me how to do this. I also learned how to have my own place as well, because I know that I had to show that I tried hard to live on my own independently as an adult at school. I even showed that I gained independence with getting around the Sutherland Campus in Peterborough due to the fact that this was where I had a group of grown-up friends who were like family.

I also moved and am now in a condo with my mom, so I am learning how to do my own schedule, laundry, and things like getting my lunch ready. I think that giving myself this independence with college and my own place has given me more freedom, it is because that I show that I can handle living on my own. I learned how to take transit to co-op when I was at college in another city. Now I have to relearn new transit routes as I have moved, and I have not taken transit since the pandemic started. Being able to come and go freely is important so I can show others that I can look after myself and find my way around in my community.

The COVID-19 pandemic has been difficult for not just me, but for everyone. I think that the reason is because the corona virus is a deadly disease, and independence has been difficult due to the fact that I can't even use public transit. During the pandemic, I was still able to go to the Abilities Centre for workouts but only if I have a doctor's note from Dr. Flood. COVID-19 was stressful because of how many times I had to follow stay-at-home orders from the Ontario Government. I had to do social groups, workouts, music lessons, soccer, baseball, rugby, archery, and writing books from home virtually, and it has been so hard for me because it is not easy to get through a lockdown as it is so isolating. In fact, during the second lockdown in 2021, I wondered if it would ever end. I realized that I also walk laps around my community and work hard on my board games and LEGO Architecture sets that I like to build from scratch to keep busy, as well as playing board games. These things kept my mind active during lockdown. I went for a walk one hour a day with my mom and lost a lot of weight doing that activity. The difficulty with COVID though was not seeing people in person and not being able to go to all my programs. I got tired easily when everything was virtual, and I found it hard to follow who is talking and who is not. I am so pleased the pandemic is over!

Not everything thought about COVID-19 has been negative; there were some positive things too. I was lucky enough to be able to continue to help with the YAC at Grandview, the AAC at Kerry's Place as well as the YAC with JaysCare. All these committees continued online so I still had a connection to my friends and the places I liked to visit. I did get my job at the start of the pandemic, but, with a few lockdowns, I had to stay home and not work. The good news is I am back and going regularly now. Most of my teams went online too so it was difficult, but we still at least got to see each other and interact doing games and exercises online.

I hope we never have another pandemic, but I would like to give so many pieces of advice to others who are struggling during the pandemic—or other times they are forced to stay at home, perhaps due to sickness or disability. I would tell them to exercise, get involved, go join committees, and, finally, make sure that they get into extracurricular activities. Getting involved during the pandemic was tough, but as long as you are fully vaccinated and keeping an eye on how you look at which extra curriculars are up for grabs, you will persevere and there is no reason to give up. Have high hopes and dream big that the sky will be the limit. I also think that if you are not active with anything, your health will struggle, you will get more anxious and stressed out, and your body will deteriorate as you get older.

Furthermore, a piece of advice I would like to share to others who are struggling is that there are ways you can look on the bright side, there are ways you can change the way you think. Look at what resources there are to choose from. You can be seen as a success story in your local community by learning that there are a variety of choices you can do to keep active and get involved to stay out of trouble. Finally, my last piece of advice I would like to say is that you can learn to teach and help others so you can work as a team during and after a pandemic.

I would like to give so many positive pieces of advice to youth who are going from adolescence into adulthood. I would tell them to find a job/career and learn how to live grown-up life independently by getting your own place, as well as learning how to cook meals from scratch in your own home. Teaching adolescents going from their teen years to adulthood can be tough sometimes. They have to learn how to do adult skills as they get older into high school. That means they have to learn to do adult living skills on their own independently so that they can start a family on their own as well. If you find the right community support (and there are many out there now), you can find ways to be successful and more involved in your community. I would also like to add that becoming an adult can be scary and tough, but if you have the right friends and support system and are involved in volunteering in your community, this will open up doors for you down the road just like it did for me.

The last thing I would like to say is that you should never give up on your dreams. I am still dreaming. There are things I cannot wait to do, like travel the world and maybe throw out the first pitch at a Toronto Blue Jays game! I also hope to go another world tour with my Mixed Ability Rugby team, maybe in Italy or Argentina! If I can do it, you can, and I know that for a fact. Remember, you are strong and can do hard things. Everything is possible.

Yogurt Parfait Recipe
By Elliot Smith

Ingredients

1 cup of plain yogurt
I scoop of granola
4-5 strawberries
Blueberries
Blackberries
Banana
Honey

Instructions

1. Wash your fruit that you are using. If you don't have any of the berries, you can use your own fruit that you have at home, like an orange, for example.
2. Add the yogurt in a glass or cup
3. Cut up the strawberries in halves.
4. Peel the banana and slice up the banana into pieces.
5. Place the washed berries and any cut fruit into the bowl with the yogurt.
6. Sprinkle the granola on top like a sundae
7. Drizzle some honey on top.
8. Ta da! You have yogurt parfait!

Working, Career, and Managing Finances
By Justin Milner

Working and volunteering is a way of life. It is the backbone of my personal, social, and overall lifestyle. My opinion is that I don't think I would be where I am today without it. Even with the extra things I do on the side. You need some sort of financial support, that's why having a career is very important to me.

Working and volunteering, you feel accomplished. Your sense of self-worth is high overall-pride is the most rewarding feeling that you can have. Not every day is going to be the best, it is what you make it. I have been working for 19 years straight. I met a lot of people, some good and some not so good, and I have learned that always do you best regardless of what others say.

The volunteering aspect, in my opinion feels like the same as working doing what you love, supporting a cause that you believe in. I know I have a lot of fun volunteering. The appreciation and the audience clapping and cheering after performances when I volunteer in theatre says it all.

I have done a lot of job interviews in my lifetime. Auditions and trying to get myself out there: I can do these now. A lot of it is terrifying, putting yourself out there in front of people, but, nine times out of ten, you may never see them again so just have fun with it.

Complex Family Dynamics—That Work!
By Eric Lauder

Good day! My name is Eric Lauder. I'm 25, I am an older brother of two siblings who are also diagnosed with ASD, and I am a full-time student at the University of Toronto. Truthfully, I can't remember when I was first diagnosed, but I remember having autism for… well, just about as long as I can remember. When I was a young kid, in either kindergarten or, like, grade one or something, the teacher asked us to count to the biggest number we could think of. Being able to see the very obvious pattern (i.e. 1, 2, 3 … 10, 20, 30 … 100, 200, 300) I got ridiculously high—almost 300, I think—and the only reason I stopped was because it was time to go home. I think that's when people began to realize I had autism, because most other kids just gave up out of boredom. I did recently get re-diagnosed in university, just a couple years ago, along with a formal depression and anxiety diagnosis, so that's cool.

Within my day-to-day life, my biggest struggle comes from needing to help care for my siblings. Our father isn't in the picture, so I need to take on a dad-esque role within the household. This includes the usual household chores (laundry, grocery shopping, cooking, cleaning, etc.) but on a magnified scale, since I also have to do these chores for others, as well. I do laundry and shopping for basically my whole family, mother included, and I cook for both my brother and me. My mom tends to do most of the cleaning, though I help where I can. I'm also responsible for taking care of my younger brother, Jacob, while our mom works. While he is 18, he is completely dependent; he can't cook, and he has the tendency to self-harm when he loses control over his emotions, and I'm, quite frankly, the only one capable of stopping him when he tries to hurt himself, since he's a pretty big guy. While my sister is somewhat more independent, she still has her own share of issues, especially considering her tendency to blow up and start fights due to her anxiety. While I understand that it's not intentional, it certainly makes my life far more stressful.

This complex relationship with my family is, undoubtedly, the greatest struggle I have with independence; although, I guess it qualifies more as co-dependence? Either way, the stress of balancing school with my home life is quite tiresome, especially considering that I am the sole driver in my household, needing to drive mom to work, ferry people to appointments, and get myself to class. This spatial aspect of independence is complex, pulling me every which way and making dealing with personal issues more difficult than it ought to be. And, of course, as the two concepts are inextricably intertwined, the same can be said about the time constraints placed upon me, eating away at my already scarce free time. Given how many assignments at school are timed and due on specific days, the challenge of life and independence comes from the struggle to maintain this school-life balance, juggling these myriad obligations with precarious mental health. All the same, I manage because I must, often at the expense of my mental health and/or sleep schedule.

In a similar vein, I would like to share a story about my experiences accessing supports at my school. We've got something called AccessAbility Services, and like the name suggests, their job is to make sure students with disabilities have proper accommodations to succeed in their classes. The services themselves are quite helpful; they can give you extra time for assignments or extra time to write an exam and can get you class notes through the use of a volunteer notetaker. The big issue with AccessAbility is the tedious process to get these supports. In my experience, I had to get and have several appointments with the school's psychologist, which is a pain because he doesn't come in very often, turning the process into a several-month-long slog. After that, I needed to have a meeting with a counselor to discuss what proper accommodations would be for me, after which point, I got access to these supports.

The issue, as highlighted above, is the annoying time and space expectations placed upon me—to prove I had a disability, they made me go out of my way, carving more time from my already packed schedule in order to get access to these supports, making me drive all the way to school—a 45 minute drive, mind you—in order to attend these meetings. There simply seems to be this idea that time is somehow less valuable for those with disabilities—that we have nothing better to do than attend all of these tedious meetings in order to prove that we need help. To make matters worse, after a couple years they revoke these supports and make you schedule another meeting with a counselor, plus bring a signed medical form from a doctor, in order to "make sure the accommodations are still sufficient." The problem being that if you don't do this, they just straight up take your accommodations.

Again, I was subjected to these tedious meetings meant only to steal my time, but this time, it's somehow worse, because they already know and have documented proof showing that I have autism but still want to schedule an appointment anyways to make sure my autism hasn't run off or anything! Worse off, they want a doctor, who I haven't even spoken to in at least 3 years, to "confirm" that I still have a disability, like their educational background allows them to know what accommodations I require better than I do! I get that it's just a way of making sure that neurotypical people don't abuse the system to get unfair access to accommodations they don't need, but, when the entire process ends up harming the very people they're supposed to be helping, then there's a significant problem that needs to be addressed.

MEATLOAF RECIPE
BY: ERIC LAUDER

A little blurb before we get to the meatloaf recipe: Those who know me know that I'm the family cook. I've gotta make big meals, preferably with a lot of leftovers, so that we've got lunch for the next day. One of my most common homemade meals is my meatloaf: just a big brick of meat, onion, and spices, perfect for filling the belly. I make it once a week, every Friday, and it's my little brother's favourite. It's (relatively) quick, easy, and tasty, which is why it's such a go-to meal for me. So, without further ado, let's get into it.

INGREDIENTS:

Approx 1 kg of ground meat (I use beef or a mix of beef and pork)
1 cup of breadcrumbs
2 eggs
1 onion, finely chopped
3 tbsp ketchup
2.5 tbsp of parsley
2 tbsp of Worcestershire sauce
3 tsp of garlic powder
1.5 tsp of Italian seasoning
1.5 tsp of salt
0.5 tsp of paprika
0.5 tsp of black pepper
A pinch of cayenne pepper, or to taste (for spiciness)
BBQ sauce for topping (I like hickory and brown sugar BBQ sauce)
Also: a really big bowl and a rectangle baking pan!

Step 1: Add everything (except BBQ sauce) into a big bowl
Step 2: Mix it up reallly good! (Also, preheat the oven to 375°F) Depending on your sensory preferences, this step might be really fun, or a total sensory nightmare. I don't have any fancy mixing tools, so I just use my bare hands to mix everything up. You'll know you're done when you've got a huge meatball that looks super uniform—should be a brownish grey, with breadcrumbs, parsley, and onion spread evenly as far as you can see.
Step 3: Move it to the pan and shape it into a brick!
Step 4: When your oven is all ready to go, you should put the meatloaf inside. When that's done make sure to wash your hands really well to get all the meaty gunk off—it might take a couple tries and a lot of scrubbing! Also make sure to set a timer for 40 minutes, since that's when we'll be doing our next step!
Step 5: After the timer goes off, put on some oven gloves, take the meatloaf out of the oven, and put your BBQ sauce on top! You can use a spoon to spread it out nice and evenly. Then, set another timer for 20 minutes and put it back in the oven!
Step 6: After timer #2 goes off, take the meatloaf out of the oven again and let it cool down for at least 5-10 minutes.

Finally, cut a slice and enjoy, preferably with a tasty side dish, like fries or taters! Feeds a whole family!

PART 4:
RELATIONSHIPS

WE TALKED

TYPICAL MISUNDERSTANDINGS:
TURNING MISSTEPS INTO MOMENTS OF GROWTH

COREY: People assuming that I'm being insensitive when my brain just can't wrap itself around certain concepts. Because they don't really click with me. Like misunderstandings due to social cues. You try to understand them, but they don't mentally click. And the people around you who do understand them stab a finger at you like you are doing something wrong. Some of them assume that you're not even trying, that you're uncaring. And it leads to conflict that doesn't need to happen because you're not trying to do that.

Because I don't get it, they'll say, "That's how it is." I need to understand. It makes it easier for me to get into the habit of not doing something, or in the habit of doing something, to make things easier for us all. And if I don't understand why it's a problem, then it might come up in some other form and I'm not gonna realize it is coming up. Then someone's gonna have to call me out again. It's just a constant cycle.

AKOSUA: I remember you talking about how upset your mother was about your response after her partner died in an accident.

COREY: Yeah, my brain couldn't click with my mother's. It's like, he's gone. Yeah, it sucks. But it's not gonna help—you stressing over it, getting upset about it, dwelling on it, getting overly depressed over it. When I don't have to, why am I called insensitive because I'm not freaking out? It doesn't make any sense. It's not gonna change anything, it's not gonna make anybody's life better, so why would I freak out about it? Why would I get overly sensitive about it? It sucks, but it is what it is, and my mom got really upset—people tend to get really upset—when I don't get all weepy and freak out about people who've passed away. And it's a conflict. It leads to anger because they think —and they talk to me and treat me like—I don't care. But the reality is I just don't feel that over-intense about it as they do.

KATHERINE: Yeah.

[…]

AKOSUA: That's a big, deep topic. Does anyone else have an example where there was a misunderstanding …

DEBBIE (Relayed by Elliot's mother, as Elliot couldn't make the meeting): When Elliot first started work, he didn't have any accommodations, and he hadn't asked for any. When he gets very overwhelmed, he listens to music: it's the only thing that will help him decompress. So he was on shift one day and had his earbuds in. He's a physical fitness

support worker, so he interacts with the public quite a bit. His supervisor came over and said, "You can't do that. You can't have buds in your ears because if somebody comes up to ask you a question, they can't talk to you and you can't help them, and that's your job."
So he tried to advocate for himself. But was having a really hard time explaining it because when he gets stressed, he has a harder time connecting his words the way he wants to. So, he wasn't able to explain that day, and I redirected him to HR. And so, he met with someone in HR but brought along the job coach he had in his previous job. They walked through why he needed the earbuds. He told them he wasn't trying to bend or disobey the rules. He told them he really needed to wear them to survive his work day.

And so, long story short, they came up with a compromise: if he is stressed on the job, he's allowed to put one button in one ear, And the other one hangs out so that he can still hear if there's any worker safety issues or clients who want to ask questions. But then he also has music going in his other ear to keep him calm.

Akosua: That's a great compromise.

Debbie: But initially he was very misunderstood. The supervisor thought he just wasn't interested in his job—that he didn't want to do his job, and he didn't want to comply with the rules. So, the big thing is this instituted a whole bunch of change at the centre he's at. And so they now do accommodation plans if employees request them, so there's actually something on file too if they're comfortable with that.

Akosua: That's fantastic. So Katherine, do you have an example?

Katherine: I've a sort of broad example. General communication. I find that communicating with someone who's neurotypical is very difficult, especially when being given a task. Typically, how we ask people to do something is sort of based around implications and assumptions because It's very polite to not directly ask someone to do something. It's sort of like skirt around it. But that doesn't work well for me. I don't think that works well for most autistic people.

Corey: No, it doesn't. I agree. Yeah, the assumptions. And just the vague way they ask is confusing. Yeah.

Katherine: I've had that happen to me all the time, especially with my mom. She tends to assume that I just know to do something when, in reality, I don't. My brain just doesn't function like that.

Corey: I can relate. My mom's the same way.

KATHERINE: Typically. It's something like cleaning the kitchen or something innocuous like that, where it's something she just assumes I should know to do it without her telling me to do it. She thinks I should automatically know, and she shouldn't have to say, "Can you please do this?"

I don't "assume" to do it. And then, we get into an argument and I say, "You never really asked me," and it sounds like I'm being pedantic because there's an assumed responsibility there to actually do it. But it's just not how my brain processes that.

COREY: Does your mom get frustrated when things aren't done in a specific way?

KATHERINE: Yes. Because typically I kind of just sit there, catatonic, next to her, awaiting instruction. Then she's upset, saying, "Why aren't you helping me?" And I don't know…

COREY: And do they all still get frustrated when they're in the middle of doing something? You're trying to help, but you don't know how they want you to help and then it just makes it more complicated.

KATHERINE: Yeah.

COREY: Yeah, my mom's the exact same way. She wants help, but she gets frustrated when people don't help her the way she wants. And she acts like everybody knows how to do what she's thinking, and it leads to arguments. Yeah. I know how that feels, too. It's so confusing. I tend to just steer clear at this point.

KATHERINE: I want to help my mom. I don't want her to have to do everything by herself. I just wish there was some more direct communication. On her part, it's sort of the politeness that stops her, I think.

COREY: Yep.

[…]

AKOSUA: Scott, you've mentioned that having face blindness gets you in trouble. Sometimes people might think you're rude, but you just didn't even recognize them, although you'd met them several times before.

SCOTT: Yes… I have an example, but it's horrible and embarrassing. So when I was in an electronic school, my friend and I used to go across the road to Burger King and have food and pull out our homework and stuff. And there were three beautiful women who worked there and the reason I remember all this episode is I wrote it down in my diary.

So, the year passed and graduation came. The night before I was going to leave Brampton, I went over to this Burger King, just to say thank you.

COREY: Okay.

SCOTT: So, yeah, I said thank you, and I had some food and then when I was leaving the Burger King, one girl rushed out behind me and said, "I want to have your baby," and I'm like, "Uhm" and I walk away. This just didn't make any sense to me. So I kept walking and years later somebody said to me that this meant that she liked me. I had no sense of that, so … wish I'd known!

I mean I thought she was beautiful, but I know from horrible experience that it's generally not a good idea for me to express interest in somebody because it ends up so embarrassing. So, maybe I missed something because I had no sense she might have had any kind of feelings or anything for me. That was one of my weirdest non-relationships.

AKOSUA: Thank you so much for getting vulnerable there. Especially sharing something that you think might be embarrassing, but I think it's something that lots of people have experienced in one way or another.

KATHERINE: That just reminded me of something that is somewhat related to Scott's story, actually.

With my friends, I haven't really understood where the boundary is between being a friend and being someone who you're in a relationship with. Because to me if we're really good friends, I'm okay with cuddling on the couch with you. I'm okay with showing affection in that way. But at a certain point, and I don't realize when it crosses that boundary, it will cross into relationship territory, and they think that we're becoming far closer than we actually are. And I lead them on in a way without realizing it. To me, it's just I'm not in a relationship with you.

You're my friend. I love you platonically. So, therefore, I wouldn't be sending a subliminal signal. If I liked you, I would say I like you in that other way.

BRIANNA: I didn't understand relationships. That's why I got pregnant so young.

Ciara: Sort of similar to what other people have touched on, me and my partner would often get into conflicts as I need a lot of clarification on things. I've said something he perceived as rude, and I want specific clarification so it doesn't happen again in the future. Often a lot of neurotypicals will assume you should already have automatically known the problem so they'll refuse to give you clarification, which just leaves me feeling very confused.

Katherine: Right.

Corey: Fair enough. Ciara, have you invented "It's Not Quite Tea" yet? For those British people like you who don't like tea–you should do that.

Katherine: Yeah!

Corey: Kind of it's not butter or yeah.

Scott: These people not liking tea. Sorry my family is British and tea was, like, default.

Akosua: She must be part French or something.

[All - sounds of laughter]

"Your Voice Matters"

Every perspective enriches the conversation. As you reflect on the ideas shared here, we encourage you to keep the dialogue alive—whether it's with your friends, family, or community. Share your thoughts, your questions, and your experiences. Together, we can create more understanding and inclusion.

Escaping Loneliness as an Autistic Person
By Ciara Freeman

Sometimes I feel like I'm an outsider looking in. Like I'm at the zoo, and I'm looking through the glass at every neurotypical person I know on the inside. They're going to parties, going for their bottomless brunches, being invited to be bridesmaids at their best friends' weddings… It looks fun, yet totally bizarre and completely alien to me.

I mean, I can make friends, and I've had some fantastic friendships, but I'm rarely, if ever, the best friend. I was always the last kid chosen for any school project or sport, and I've always been the one not invited to something all my other friends have been invited to.

I don't think this is an uncommon way to feel when you're autistic, but it comes with a great deal of loneliness. When you learn about autism, it's common to hear about how we have difficulty maintaining friendships and meaningful relationships, but I don't think it's so common to hear about how that makes us feel and the effects that has on us as people.

Humans, generally, are social creatures. While a lot of autistic people aren't very social, I definitely am. I absolutely adore being around people, and I struggle mentally when I'm on my own for too long. When I'm spending time with people, I never want that time to end, even though my social battery runs low pretty fast.

I really love having a brain that thinks differently to others, but it comes with a level of disconnect with other people. I spend a lot of time trying to understand the unspoken neurotypical rules of socialising that everyone except me seems to be able to automatically grasp. I'm also naturally a chronic overthinker so a lot of this has devolved into quite severe social anxiety for me over the years.

I always worry about what I'm saying, how I say it, how it will be perceived. If someone wants me to do something, I will need hyper specific clarification on each step so I can be sure I won't do it wrong. I'm terrified of messing up. I'm scared of being too much like me because I know that I'm a pretty weird person. I have obscure interests and a sense of humour most people don't get. And as soon as I get comfy with someone, I'm a chronic oversharer too.

With all of this in mind, I've decided several times that trying to make friends is too much effort. I can't pretend to be someone I'm not, and being myself is terrifying too, but I crave connection and company.

As soon as I finished school, I became self-employed working from home. This was fantastic! I could stay where I feel the comfiest and safest *ALL* the time! When the pandemic happened, lockdown was a breeze— I'd been a shut-in for years already.

But I was lonely. Staying in my cozy bubble also meant I had no opportunities to meet anybody, so I didn't. Loneliness isn't an unfamiliar feeling to me; I've felt like a total outcast since I first started school, so I got used to spending a lot of time alone. After all of that time spent by myself, I grew up to have a hatred of being in my own company, my own brain exhausts me when I'm the only person it can talk to.

I was desperate for something to change, but I didn't know how to change things. Most people find friendship from school or work, or some sort of group activity, but school didn't work out for me. And now I worked from home, and the idea of trying to fit into a group and convince a group of people I'm somehow not the weird lil' goblin girl I am— well that was extremely intimidating.

After a few more years of this, I finally found the courage and confidence to join a drama group; that's when I realised I didn't know how to talk to people. Talking to people had always been scary, sure, but I could make conversation. Now, after so many years of being by myself with only my brain and my partner to keep me company, I realised how bad my social skills had gotten. I guess socialising isn't like riding a bike where you'll always remember how to do it—not for me anyway. I learnt that being able to talk to people was a skill that I needed to use regularly to be able to stay good at it.

The first few weeks of going to this drama group, my anxiety ate me up. Everyone seemed so fun and friendly! I desperately wanted to get to know them all, but I'd try to talk to someone, and I'd freeze up. I didn't know how to be myself. I couldn't think of anything to say, I wouldn't be able to think of the words. People get this idea of me that I'm quiet and shy, and that couldn't be further from the truth. It will just take me months before I can get to the point of being myself around you, and most people aren't that patient.

At least with a weekly drama group, nobody had to be patient with me, because everyone was there every week anyway. Eventually, I started to find my voice a bit more, and, by show week, I had gained so much confidence, I was starting to crack jokes, I didn't feel like so much of a weirdo outcast, and I was beginning to make friends for the first time in six years.

Then show week ended, and the group split up over the summer, and I was alone again for a few months. That was really difficult for me. All I wanted to do was hang out with these people I still barely knew really, but I wanted to know them better. I would get very sad thinking about how I so desperately wanted to befriend these people, but they didn't feel the same way. Which is understandable, they still didn't know me, and they had their own friendship circles already. They didn't have that same desperation for connection like me, and none of them knew my internal struggle for it.

When the group started up again, my social skills had disappeared again over the summer. I was starting at square one, not being able to talk to anybody and freezing up when I tried. I just had to slowly relearn this skill again bit by bit every week.

What I haven't mentioned yet is the magical potion I'd discovered that would make all of that struggle go away—the potion that would let me be myself, this handy thing I could drink, and I'd suddenly be able to talk to people: alcohol.

Alcohol was the only thing that would help. I'd be confident, I would know what to say, how to say it, when to say it. I wouldn't overthink every single word and how I'd be perceived. Everything came naturally to me when I had a drink or two in my system.

It wasn't a solution though, obviously. The next day I would be fighting off panic attacks trying to remember every little thing I'd said, trying to figure out if I had embarrassed myself. Oh no, suddenly everybody knows how weird I am, and then next time they see me I'll be this quiet person who can't talk again, and then they'll all think I'm even weirder.

Shit.

Alcohol fed my anxiety, but it let me have what I wanted the most, which was to not feel lonely, or outcast. It allowed me to feel a part of something, welcome. I felt like I could no longer be myself at all if I was sober, like I had this whole other person just locked inside of me, and a glass of wine was the key to let them out to play.

This is the reason why I think autism can be a blessing and a curse. I like to see the positives in everything, or if there has to be a negative, I at least try to make something positive out of that. But the truth is, if I wasn't autistic, my liver would likely be thanking me because I wouldn't need alcohol to be more content in my own company. I'm sure, without autism, I probably wouldn't have this same deep craving for connection.

But then again… I wouldn't be me either. Honestly, I'd probably be a lot more boring. I mean, yeah, I'm weird, but at least nobody can call me boring.

Finding a Path from Being Used to Being Part of a Community
By Justin Milner

My whole life, I felt outside right from the beginning. I don't remember much from my childhood. I'm not sure why. I do have memories of different things and events but not too much. I was born into a very dysfunctional family, with my father and mother working many different jobs throughout my childhood. I never really had grandparents—my grandfather disowned my mother when I was about eight years old, and I have not seen him since.

I was often neglected, left alone for hours, sometimes even days, at a time. Isolated. My younger brother was always out with friends; well, I didn't have any. I endured a lot, from body shaming to condescension. Everything I said and did was always wrong. As I think back, everything I did in life was seen as a waste of time when I was a child.

Growing up, I was in special education classes. Every two or three years, I would have to change schools because my program ended. This didn't give me a chance to make friends or be social with anyone. I was always told that I would never go to college, get a job, drive, or ever have a "normal life." My whole life, I had difficulties making friendships as I don't have a knack for social skills. It was always a challenge for me to have conversations with people, finding it hard to read and act—displaying those "social manners." I don't feel emotions in the same way, and I've sometimes been called insensitive and uncaring to the needs of other people. Also, I've been told I have an unemotional style of speaking.

I'm not gonna lie: I did have behaviour issues when I was a kid, often having mental breakdowns and fits if something was out of place, or I didn't get my own way.

Relationships. I do as much as possible to avoid them. I still get called "retarded," and it doesn't even bother me anymore. I was always made to feel that I was a minority being shunted off from others almost as if they were being protected from me and others like me. Sad part is I have always figured they do it because it makes them feel better about themselves.

My romantic relationships with different people over the years have been a bit rocky. In fact, a recent relationship I had was a bit strange. I was accused of cheating on her all the time only to find out later she had cheated on me several times. I never knew what gaslighting was until then, even had a few nervous breakdowns. It was emotionally draining.

About ten-ish years ago, I felt like the friends I had were just using me for my money and car. Most of my early 20s were just a blur sometimes, with me not even remembering what I did for days at a time. I was getting backstabbed so badly over the years, and the problem was I couldn't say NO. I was involved in a lot of illegal activities; it was getting bad. I realized I was going to end up like a lot of people I knew—in prison or dead. I think the last straw was when I got a call from a friend saying I owe this other friend over a thousand dollars from a swing I allegedly broke six months earlier. I was not going to give any more of my money. I was already scammed out of tens of thousands of dollars on other people buying cars, vet bills, drugs—the list goes on. I felt that I would never recover financially.

When I started to ask questions, I was told not to worry about it. At the time, I was right; no one cared about me or my feelings. I know that I should have put myself first. I was also the guy who did nothing but bad and wondered why my life sucked. Every time something good happened, something bad was always waiting for me. I decided to make a New Year's resolution to alter my life for the greater and to be more positive. I was unhappy with the direction I was going in. I needed a change, I said to myself, "I'm just trying to be a better person."

A long time ago, I would have never believed that people can change until I did it. It's a lot of hard work, but it can be done. I used to have this friend who got picked on all the time. Being called bad names, being made fun of—everything would happen to this guy, so he would message all his friends, losing it. He would go from 0-100 just like that and there was nothing I could say to calm him down. I remember coming home after a long day to see over 80 messages telling me how much of a horrible person I was. There was a lot of name calling. I was terrified and at that point, I had to give up on him. The aftermath was not good, and to this day, I still get anxiety when I get texts, e-mails, and messages, which is not healthy.

The only phone calls I used to get were "Can I get a ride?" or "Can you do me a favour?" I believe this is why I lost a lot of friends and people in my life as this made me hate driving people around for free. I felt more like I'm being used than anything else. As of today, I'm in a much better place. I have friends that care, a full-time job, volunteer jobs, and so many projects on the go.

Over the years, I had 26 interviews for full-time jobs and several different jobs within the company and the store I've worked at since I was 16. All these interviews and I got no luck moving forward from where I started at age 16. The last interview I had in November, 2020 was a trip. I was told I was not a leader, and no one wanted me there, even part time. It's very heartbreaking to me walking in every day knowing the manager at the time didn't want me there. It is very hurtful being very loyal after all these years. Yes, I want to move forward, and I felt like I was wasting my time, but I didn't want to stop fighting for better.

I never gave up, and, three years later, I was offered an apology and a full-time job, I know it would have taken some time, but I never gave up hope. I remember when I started there, I had to give up a lot of holidays, family gatherings, birthdays, and weekends—it was a challenge. I was in high school at the time, doing homework and assignments, staying up until 1am in the morning just to finish everything. I was in school for seven hours and then work for seven hours; it was tiring. But in the end, I ended up paying for college all on my own. It worked out very well for me.

Either way, my life was moving forward. I have done a lot of cool things so far in my life, like skydiving, white water rafting, kayaking, zip lining, and boxing, and I've seen a great deal of amazing places. I usually wake up and say *I want to do this*, and I go out and do it. I was even a contestant on Canada's Got Talent in 2011! I didn't get very far with it, but I still try new things. Like background acting in a survival film and television shows. I was background in the movie *It* in 2017 an *It* and *It Chapter 2* in 2019; they are the biggest projects I have done so far.

For me I find it difficult being on the autism spectrum, especially being high-functioning autistic. I'm often overlooked, unappreciated, and not taken seriously, which makes life that much harder for me. I have always felt different and often discriminated against. A lot of people don't know how to talk or even act in front of someone on the spectrum. For me, anyways, just be yourself.

I used to care about what people thought of me. If someone didn't like me, I would just stay in bed and want to die. After a while, I thought I just could not do that anymore. There were people out there that did like me. I don't have a lot of friends, I don't really have anyone to call if I'm feeling down, if I need support, or anything, but I am used to being alone and by myself. If I like myself, that's all that really matters to me.

People make fun of me all the time for posts on social media a lot, and, to be honest, I use it as a therapy tool. I would wake up every day wishing I wasn't here anymore; social media sure did help me. It gave me a place that I can look at and see the people that care for me, to show me that life is worth fighting for and most importantly to prove to myself people are interested in me.

I joined Autism Home Base in May of 2019. It's a charity that runs programs for adults on the autism spectrum. I was asked by a friend if I would attend a Durham College Transition event with him, and, at the last minute, he canceled. I wasn't going to attend, but I thought I might as well go, and I am so glad I did. They had booths set up all the way around the room for different organizations, most of them were employment agencies, and I saw one for Autism Home Base. I asked a friend who is a member of AHB about it, and he happened to be at the event: he said it's an amazing group. So, I decided to check it out to see how it was.

The first event I ever went to was a games group. For the first time in a long time, I felt like I belonged here. At the time, I didn't have many friends and was often alone, so it just felt right becoming a member. Since that day I have met a lot of great people, had a blast, and even started volunteering my free time there as well. Joining Autism Home Base was one of the best decisions I have made in my life so far.

Through AHB, I met Akosua who ran a creative writing group called Creative Expressions. She suggested we put our stories together to create a book. A lot of family and friends were against me writing this book, giving a lot of different reasons I should not share my story. For a while, I wasn't even sure about myself again, I did cry a lot when I was writing, and I did leave a lot of things out, but overall writing has been uplifting. I got a lot off my chest that have been eating away at me for so long.

I can't change what happened, but I certainly change what is going to happen. If I can help someone going through a tough time, that's awesome. My experience is advice. My main message is sometimes you can't choose where your life is, but you can change your future by adjusting the little things. I am still working on myself every day, and, trust me, I made the best of it. My life is better than it was ten, and even five and two years ago. I finally found a way to be the person I've always wanted to be, the person I wished I was all those years ago.

Sobeys Big Ride for Heart and Stroke Fundraiser in 2019. As a group we raised over $3,000 for Heart and Stroke Research, and, out of that, I raised $1,680.

Autism Home Base Art project at the Robert McLaughlin Museum "Meet Me At The Hub" what are you proud of, what are you afraid of, and what makes you unique.

Olaf and Ozzie—Making My Home Feel Full
By Corey Kearns

I got Ozzie when I was about 21 years old and he has changed my life a lot. I got him from a friend of my mum, who got him from an older couple. That couple got him after family members moved in then abandoned him in their basement. Ozzie is a very social dog with a persistent personality, he loves baths, and he's great with kids as well as little dogs. Ozzie isn't picky at all—in fact, once, when the vet said I had to give him medication, I didn't have the problems they warned me about. Ozzie ate the pills straight from my hands like they were treats. Ozzie is a fairly old dog right now, but he still has lots of puppy energy.

I got Olaf from my cousin because their older cat was losing their fur from Olaf's antics, or at least that's my understanding. Olaf is a very chill cat—you can hold him upside down, and he just chills hanging up there. You can hold him like a baby, and he will just lay there, content. My cousin taught him to grip things that you bring close to him with his paws when you hold him like a baby, too. Olaf is a very affectionate kitty, but he can also be a real jerk. Sometimes he will scratch a wall or the couch and stare at you while doing it. If you chase him out of the room, he will stop when you stop and then follow you back to resume what he was doing. He isn't scared of spray bottles, and he loves his cat nip.

Olaf and Ozzie are very much like brothers; they eat each other's food, are jealous of the attention the other gets, and they over toys. Both my pets have played a huge part in helping me climb out of the shell I grew up in. They have made a huge difference in helping me reconnect with my emotions after the group homes. I love my pets. They are my best friends and make my home feel full.

Watching People—They Make It All Look So Easy!
By Scott R. Dawson

It has been said that everyone has a purpose in life, even if it is only to be a horrible example of What Not to Do. That is part of why I am writing this essay: to show what it feels like to be unsuccessful at social connection… and to offer some hope.

It's all part of the long journey to figure out who and what I am. But it starts long before any conscious thoughts about romance…

Around age four, I remember looking out the window watching the big kids go off to kindergarten and wondering what it would be like. After my fifth birthday, I found that the reality of kindergarten was not as great as my hopes. Bullying started then and would not stop for many years. But I survived kindergarten and entered grade one.

One day in grade one, they came and took me from class. They walked me to another classroom full of bigger kids. I was to continue in grade two. I don't know why they did this, but it set up the rest of my school career so that I was always smaller, weaker, and less developed than those around me. For a kid already bullied, this was a disaster.

The summer I turned seven, we moved to a new town. I hoped that my bad reputation would be left behind, and it seemed to work. I settled into grade three and progressed through public school. Things went along as well as they could until grade seven. Then I entered hell. Grades seven and eight were held in a different school apart from the neighbourhood public schools. All grade seven and eight students in town were bussed to a single school, and it was like *Lord of the Flies*. The bullying ramped up, and I spent my spare time hiding, either in the woods or in the library.

The other bad part was physical education. I was thrown into team sports I did not understand and could not play. But they did not teach the games; they just assumed that we already knew how to play them. The other kids didn't want me to be there, and I didn't want to be there. I would have been quite happy doing gymnastics and other solo exercises; instead, the forced team sports taught me shame about my physicality and my body and reinforced my sense of inferiority.

Despite this chaos, puberty happened, and I became aware of girls. By the spring of grade eight, I was thinking about them.

I'm pretty sure that I must have expressed interest in girls, but I learned quickly that this would only lead to more bullying and ostracism. Before I was a teenager, I learned that I had to be careful not to express any interest in anyone, lest I be slapped down.

However, near the end of grade eight, one girl actually asked me out. No-one had ever done this before; I thought it was some new and cruel form of mockery. I turned her down. Later, at grade eight graduation, my parents met her and said, "What were you thinking?" And much, much later, I ran into her on Facebook and apologized.

Along came high school: grade nine in a new school. The wretchedness of physical education continued: being trampled while playing rugger, being picked last for games I couldn't do, wrecking my knee in the gym.

In English class in grade nine, I was writing stories about the nobility of suicide. Socially, I wasn't bullied as much, but that was the only improvement. I was pressed into admitting interest in someone I had only looked at briefly from a distance, who turned out to be a boy. I suspect I was thought to be gay after this, and any chances I might have had at a date vanished.

After grade nine, I was able to leave the shame of physical education behind. The girls still weren't interested in me, but at least I was left alone. In that place and time, if a boy liked girls, he was "straight," and all was good. If he liked boys, he was "gay" and was mocked. There were no other choices.

I knew I wasn't gay, because I liked girls much too much. So, therefore, I must have been straight, right?

There was no cultural space for those who were, in the words of Umair Haque, "not straight, but not gay either." In grade eleven, I was doing paintings of myself dressed in finery that was far beyond anything any boy wore. But there was no cultural path to there, so it remained a daydream.

During high school, I had hopeless crushes on several girls, including *that* girl, you know the one: the unattainable girl every school has. She was smart, sexy, athletic, a straight-A student, *and* a cheerleader. But the crushes put me in a kind of tunnel vision. The girls I crushed on weren't interested in me, and I don't know whether anyone else was.

By this time, there was a kind of learned helplessness in me, I assumed I never had a chance and never tried. Not just dates, but also things like looking for work, or going on trips the school offered, or other extra-curricular activities. I read of ecological design from California, but it never occurred to me that going there would somehow be possible. I just drew and wrote stories.

There was also the eternal task of staying on guard and making sure I didn't say or do the wrong thing and seem creepier than I was.

I have a fragmentary memory of inviting various friends, including my crush, to a get-together at my parents' house and having them drop out one by one, until I had to cancel the event. The crush was the only one who hadn't cancelled, and I really didn't want it to be creepy, so I had to call her up to apologize and cancel.

I have another memory of going to a house party near the end of high school. Mostly, I remember how odd it seemed to see these people outside of school. It was a pool party, and I was careful not to look at the girls too much, for fear of being creepy.

I had no dates through high school, and I went to prom alone.

Only when I went to university and, later, college did things start to open up. Still had crushes on various girls (also had a crush on one guy).

And one fine day in college, I was even unexpectedly kissed! Somehow this girl I semi-liked ended up hanging out with me, and we went to the apartment where I was renting a room. She surprised me in the elevator with a kiss. I was very startled, and it took me a moment to realize what had happened. This in spite of the fact that we'd passed through the mall, where friends of my roommate had joked, "Got some action tonight?"

I was studying electronics and was sure that my chosen field of study didn't increase my attractiveness. But it was fun and interesting, and held the possibility of a job at the end. But that was also the time of my greatest regret.

During the summer between second and third year of electronics school, I was actually visiting someone I really liked, and at a crucial moment, I almost asked her out on a date. For a brief moment I agonized on a knife-edge between confidence and unworthiness… and unworthiness won. I didn't ask her out, and there was never another chance.

My second greatest regret was not going to art school. Mom said that I should have, but I didn't because I couldn't imagine how I might get a job and support myself afterwards. The social complexities were beyond my imagination. Not going to art school after high school is my second-greatest regret.

At the end of third year, I was about to graduate from electronics school with a diploma in electronics engineering technology. My friend and I had been spending a lot of time at a Burger King near his apartment, taking breaks from studying.

Three beautiful women worked there. We were glad to see them when we ordered our food, but my friend had a girlfriend, and I was careful to be friendly yet distant. After all, hitting on someone at work, when they can't get away, is a Very Bad Idea.

At the end of school, we graduated, and I decided to pay one final visit to the Burger King to say thank you before moving back to my hometown. I said hi to the women and thanked them, got my food and ate it, then left. As I crossed the parking lot, one woman came running out of the restaurant, saying, "I wanted your baby!" This made no sense to me and was even a little scary. I… continued walking.

It was only much much later that someone told me that that meant she might have been interested in me. I had no sense of anything at the time.

I returned to my hometown and found a job in electronics. I made friends there and worked there for a few years.

One time, while visiting another country, I went to a house party. A girl rushed up to me, gave me a hug, and said, "I'm so glad I don't have to have anything to do with you!" After some confusion, the host and I established that she'd been afraid that she *was promised as a sexual favour to the visitor.* I was horrified at the idea. Understandably, I never saw her again, but the experience was so odd that I soon left.

In 1989, I moved to another city. After some false starts, I got a job at the company I would be involved with for most of the next eighteen years. I settled in there fairly rapidly, working on the electronic production line.

To me, that company was notable for two things: the number of languages spoken there, and the number of beautiful women working there.

That company was where I first met a lot of people from Eastern Europe. I heard languages new to me there and made friends.

There were three women there who stood out to me in memory.

Two were friends and hung around together. One of them was tall and slender and Portuguese, and she dazzled me. Even through the crush, though, I had a sense that she wasn't really my type, so I never seriously considered doing anything more. Her friend was shorter and curvier and Italian, and also attractive, but I tended to be distracted by the first woman.

One time, I was walking through the office and was surprised by them at the door to the production floor. I had no preconceptions and was simply happy to see them. I smiled and said, "Hi," and went on my way. As I walked onto the production floor, I heard one of them say, "He's not usually like that…"

The other woman was the daughter of a lady I worked with on the floor. I got along well with the lady, and, one summer, her gorgeous daughter came to work at the company. I was smitten. Massive crush. We actually got along pretty well, and she and her mom and I would eat lunch together in the summer sun out in the picnic area at work.

But again, I was cautious, because of the usual fear of creepiness, and also because I was 27 going on 28, and she was 19 going on 20. It was on the edge of being creepy anyways.

Then one day, the mom mentioned in passing that her daughter broke up with her last boyfriend because he couldn't dance. I was crushed, because I couldn't dance either. Adding in the age difference and potential creepiness, I knew it was not to be.

After the summer was over, the daughter went on her way, and I never saw her again.

(In retrospect, I should have said something like, "I can't dance either, but I'm willing to learn…" But that's hindsight.)

Around this time, I started going to counselling. This counselling started out as the usual kind of counselling aiming to help me deal with things like my sister and mom dying, but got deeper.

It involved a lot of bodywork. This was where I discovered something that I did not know was even missing from my life: physical touch.

Things as simple as hugs turned out to be grounding and calming to me. I learned what massage was. I realized that I had been going to get unnecessary haircuts simply because when they washed my hair, it was a scalp massage.

In 1991, I decided to go back to school, to study animation. I applied almost on a whim but got accepted. I left my electronics job and moved to a new place in another nearby city. And there I was, in a new school facing the world of art. I made new friends. I also started tackling some of the greatest challenges of my life, artistic ones that dated back to early high school. I wrote new stories and drew new drawings.

We had a life-drawing class. It was taught by a man who radiated inner peace in a way I have seldom met. It also had nude models; this was a first for me. But I discovered that once I slipped into what I call 'the art state of mind', any weird feelings about the nudity vanished. I mentally disappeared in a way, and there was only the drawing process and the paper.

This art state of mind was even strong enough to overcome sexual interest. One week we had an extremely appealing model: short, blonde, and curvy. She was very distracting as we got set up to draw, but once we started drawing and got into the art state of mind, all that was forgotten.

At the end of the drawing session, we shook ourselves and came back to the normal world. The model picked up her robe and vanished into the next room. We packed up. I was very interested in the model, but I can't think of anything much creepier than hitting on the nude model in one's art class, so I put the idea aside. Besides, we had to rush to the next class.

Sometime later, I boarded a crowded bus leaving the college. I had just taken up a standing position behind the rear door, and was thinking, "I'm too tall to look out the main windows, and too short to look out the upper windows" (the bus had an extra row of small windows above the main ones), when I heard a voice behind me.

"Remember me?"

Somehow, I realized the voice was directed at me, and I turned. A seated blonde woman was looking at me. I must have had a look of confusion on my face, because she added, "You probably don't recognize me with my clothes on."

Now I was really confused. We sorted out that she was the model from my art class, and we talked a little as the bus went down to the train station.

I don't remember what happened after that. This is typical.

All was not lost though; the following spring I actually started going out with one of the members of our little group of students who used to hang around in the lounge near the animation studios. This relationship was an eye-opener in so many ways. It didn't last, but I am so very grateful for it. At age 29, I actually had a girlfriend!

Eventually, I decided to leave animation school and go back to work. I had only been away from work for 11 months, so my old job accepted me back with a gap, and I continued working there for over ten years.

Leaving animation school may have been my third great regret.

Sometime after I returned to work, I continued with counselling, and my counsellor recommended that I go to group counselling, to teach me about being social. This turned out to be the most difficult thing I have done in my life, more difficult than any job or university course. There was raw emotion, and, at times, I was overwhelmed and had to hide. But the counselors were always there to support me and the others.

There was a week-long retreat. I remember having an argument with a woman. It took all of my strength to do it, because I was certain that I would be emotionally destroyed. One of the other men was at my back, physically supporting me. And one of the other women was at the woman's back, supporting her. And the counsellors were there, helping us through it.

Intensity has always been difficult for me. Intense tastes, noises, other things. When I was a teenager, if people were arguing on TV, I would go upstairs to read.

In my forties, I discovered that many people could remember and instantly see the identity of someone in their face. I have always had to deduce who people are by putting together contextual clues like expected location, voice, gait, clothing, hairstyle.

A little research led me to "prosopagnosia," or face blindness. I had always stood a little back, taking a little time to figure out who people were when I met them. And during school, it always took me about three months to start to know who people were in a class… and then a month later the class would end.

Perhaps this distance affected how people perceived me in school.

But that wasn't the only thing. I was looking for books on 3D visualization, and I found Temple Grandin's book *Thinking in Pictures*. It wasn't about visualization specifically, but it was about growing up on the autism spectrum. And as I read, I became more and more puzzled. Why did her experiences—things like being comforted by weight on you—seem so familiar?

I talked to my counselors. I have never been formally diagnosed as being on the spectrum, but they definitely think it's possible.

At age 49, I went back to school again. The stress of school, plus external family events, led to an actual mental breakdown during second year. I went to the hospital and, for the first time, was prescribed antidepressants.

It was like a grey tint over my inner world lifted. My usual dark thoughts became much less frequent, and I stopped having nightmares (I'd been having them pretty much every other night for as long as I could remember).

I could lift my head and take a better look at things.

After school, I moved around the province and eventually ended up at the job I have now. It's assembly-line work, simple and repetitive, which I find strangely soothing at times. I can think of other things while working, like stories and drawings.

I joined a writing group and actually got stories a) finished and b) published!

And even in the past few months, there are hints of newness. And as with the counselling, it involves 'something different', not 'something more'.

Among the vast quantities of dating advice for men, most of which gives the Usual Advice of getting fit etc., I have recently found some essays that point in a different and more subtle direction. Maybe women aren't concerned with physical appearance as much as men are. Maybe they can view us more positively once they get to know us.

Getting to know us… this is where social skills matter so critically. And this is where the most difficult things in my life to learn have been.

Here are two essays. In the first, Madelaine Hanson writes, "Your Girlfriend or Wife Probably Didn't Think You Were Sexy Immediately":

https://madelainehanson.medium.com/your-girlfriend-or-wife-probably-didnt-think-you-were-sexy-immediately-but-she-didn-t-settle-0917cf16caca

This essay addresses how women evaluate men. Appearance is not the first criterion; the first thing is safety. Are you safe to be around? The second criterion is, are you socially competent? Appearance comes afterwards, followed by other concerns.

And that social competence is the critical thing. I *know* I have been socially incompetent. Maybe I couldn't help it, what with the face blindness and all.

The second essay is Mona Lazar's "How to Be Attractive Even If You're Ugly":

https://medium.com/the-soulciety/how-to-be-attractive-even-if-youre-ugly-7cb5af6921da

This essay speaks about seduction. Now, to me, "seduction" had a vaguely sleazy connotation, full of unpleasant stereotypes and manipulation. But Mona has a different view. She states, "The most seductive thing you can do is this: study people, find out what they're missing, and give it to them."

That doesn't mean lie to them, it doesn't mean trick them, manipulate them, etc. It means listen to them and put yourself in their shoes, see the world from their perspective. It actually means love them enough to understand them.

This is a very personal, intimate way of relating to another. It involves getting up close to another person, in a psychological sense, close enough to perceive them. It requires setting aside one's own fears and internal distractions.

And for a person on the autistic spectrum, this can be oddly difficult. Learning to get close to people and perceive them was a big part of the counselling I took. Even looking in someone's eyes was difficult and could be disturbing.

So, seeing these essays is strangely reassuring. You don't have to worry so much about being conventionally good-looking or rich, if you can deal with the social skills.

My Mom is Number One!
By Elliot Smith

I mentioned in the section on passions that I love my pets: I have a pet rabbit named Sandy who is eight years old. He is a lop ear rabbit. I love him, and he cuddles with me. He is my therapy pet, and he gets along with my Maine Coon, Casper, really well. We adopted Casper from the Humane Society. He is four years old now. I love him, and he purrs all the time.

However, the most important relationship I have is with my mom. My mom is my cheerleader and my number one supporter. My mom never gives up on me and always is by my side. Many times, I have had meltdowns and just wanted to give up as I get so frustrated because others don't always understand me, but she keeps pushing me to work harder and to do my best.

I did not think I could finish high school, but my mom never gave up on me and made sure I got the right support. I was able to get the autism team to help me, and they found me my best ever EA. His name is JC, and he is why I finished high school. I graduated with a diploma, and I went on to do an extra year of high school in the School to Work Program. I then went on to college where I graduated with honours and got an award for highest overall grades in the CICE program from Fleming College. During this time, I also lived in residence and most people thought I would not be able to do it, but I did. I had Community Living workers that would come in and teach me how to clean, how to take the bus to co-op and how to just have fun! My mom helped set up all this support so I could make it, and I did!

I have always loved sports, and, since I volunteered at the Abilities Centre for seven years, they finally hired me after I graduated college. I am a Physical Fitness and Literacy Associate and help to keep the gym clean, set up for fitness classes and help members when they come with questions. I also was hired by the Centre to be a Mixed Ability Sports Facilitator, where I teach coaches how to be trained in Mixed Ability Sport. I love it, and I get paid for it!

I joined the Oshawa Vikings Mixed Ability team during this time and became the team co-captain for our Men's Mixed Ability Rugby team. I have competed two times in Ireland and have become a World Cup Finalist! All this time, my mom was right behind me cheering me on. My mom and I wrote two children's books after these tours. One is called *Mateo's Mixed Ability Match,* and the other one is called *Elliot's Excellent MARI's match.* I sell these books and go to lots of events and schools to do readings. All the money goes to help Mixed Ability Rugby at our club. It was fun writing these books as my mom and I wrote them together, so she would write some sentences, then I would write some, and we kept doing this until we finished the story.

My mom is the best because she drives me everywhere, even though I could take the bus if I wanted too. She helps me on the drives, and we practice social skills on the way whether I am going to soccer, baseball, rugby, or archery. She also takes me to all my committee meetings like at the Rugby Club for Board of Directors and the Youth Advisory Council for Grandview and JaysCare. She also gives me jobs around the house and teaches me how to be more independent. Because of my mom, I have my own bank card, do my own shopping, and do our laundry.

My mom is the most important person to me. I love my grandparents too and my uncles and cousins, but my mom is number one. She loves me and supports me no matter what, even when I make mistakes. We all need a mom like her so we can all be kind to one another and so we can be the best that we can be.

Relationship with the Education System
By Katherine Layne

As a child with special needs, I found myself constantly put into situations I didn't understand and lacked the ability to properly handle. This made the world seem like a horribly unpredictable place, lacking any sort of certainty. Things seemed to just happen around me with no sort of rhyme or reason, and I was supposed to simply understand these things. Through body language, social cues, and unspoken rules, completely unknowable forces to me, guidelines I knew existed but had absolutely no comprehension of. This extremely confused experience that defined my childhood was supposedly brought to a conclusion with my diagnosis at age 6.

I was diagnosed with Asperger's Syndrome, a long outdated and inaccurate diagnosis which only served to confuse things further. It was an answer that served to only stimulate further questioning. I knew I was different, and I knew that members of my family had dissenting opinions about what caused the differences. My stepfather and my mother supported me, even with a limited understanding of disabilities, although my biological father did not support the diagnosis. He believed it was a disability of intellect, and that in some way, it meant he had failed as a parent to raise a child with autism, so he denied there was anything different about me. Through the varied reactions by my parents, I learned that this was nothing to scoff at, it meant something. Primarily, it meant that I had a quality that separated me from other children. Although my primary question still remained unanswered.

I am different. But what does it mean to be "different"?

My confusion seemed to be quelled by my first experience with any sort of Special Educational treatment. In my first elementary school, there was an EA who managed the children with IEPs. It was a small school, so there were only 3-4 of us from what I remember. She calmed my nerves surrounding my "differences" by not treating me differently at all. Her speech lacked the same patronizing tone I was used to from adults, and I felt as though when I spoke, she listened. I think it was through attentive listening that she was able to understand my needs. Through this, she was able to understand that I needed to be treated differently, but that I hated the feeling of being pandered to. So, she would devise perfect ways to strike a balance between accommodation and keeping me feeling as though my intelligence was being respected. I remember when I felt anxious or restless in class, she would send me to the office to deliver "documents", which were typically just blank pieces of paper. This was a perfect system, because it met my needs as a student and didn't cause a scene or single me out in class. Particularly, I enjoyed it because I felt as though it created a ruse of importance on my part; I delivered the documents, and I was good at it. The accommodations and slight confidence boost made this time period some of my most productive years as a student.

This period of stability and self-assurance would be shortlived. When I was eight years old, I moved schools, and the sense of comfortable self-understanding I had developed quickly eroded away. Due to the drastic change in environment and people around me, the sense of uncertainty became extremely prevalent once more. I had gone from an isolated life in the country, living alone with my mother, surrounded by woods for acres, to living in a crowded subdivision with my stepfather, surrounded by houses on all sides. I felt eyes on me at all times because of this. The sense of surveillance was bolstered by the 'new kid in town' factor I had.

My change in schools seemed to also mark a change in my social awareness. As I aged, I became far more aware of people's perceptions of me, that my differences were noticed by others, especially children. I was made a part of the Special Ed classroom. This was colloquially dubbed the "Sped" room by other students, which became my first brush with systematic bullying. Typically, it was just jabs at my intelligence, which I was able to quickly grow accustomed to. In fact, I became somewhat disappointed with their lack of creativity. You can only be called the same three slurs so many times before they become mundane. Although, the truly interesting instances would be when students chose to pick fights with me. I disliked fighting and typically wouldn't retaliate, opting to simply inform a teacher once the beating had subsided. These early experiences isolated me from my peers indefinitely.

The educators who operated the Special Ed class, I think, believed they were helping us, although, in reality, they were only stifling us. They used behavioral therapy methods to teach us how to not be autistic, using charts, boards, and posters as a sort of propaganda to constantly instill the sense of conformity. They allowed fidgeting, although, only in controlled amounts, and children who were non-verbal were treated as lesser. On multiple occasions, I would suffer from mental breakdowns due to overstimulation, and, instead of accommodating my needs, they would opt to invalidate my emotions. Instead of allowing me to discreetly exit class when I became overwhelmed, they would create a scene out of it, resulting in me not asking for help. I would rather just suffer through another panic attack silently so as not to fuel the bullying.

Here at this school, I was introduced to the five-point scale of emotions: a tool originally devised for the purpose of assisting autistic students in communicating their emotions to educators. However, my experience with this scale was marked by horrible misuse and misunderstanding. I feared this scale as a child, as it was used by my educators not as a tool of understanding but as a cudgel of invalidation. The way they achieved this was applying it improperly when I was having a reaction to something. They would rate my reaction on the scale and determine whether the severity of my reaction matched the severity of the scenario.

And if it didn't—in their opinion—they would explain to me that I was, for example, having a "five level reaction to a one level scenario." A premise which functioned to completely disconnect me from my feelings, however real they felt to me.

These experiences from middle school greatly affect me today and how I experience my own emotions and misunderstand social cues. As someone with autism, it is extremely difficult to make friends at times, at least with neurotypical people. So, I found when I was in middle school, that I made friends with other children who were in the Special Ed, class as they usually had no reason to bully me. Because of that, I developed a sense of solidarity with other people who were neurodivergent, something which I still feel today.

When I meet a new person, and I sense that they're most likely like me in that way, I tend to be more drawn to them, and it's usually far easier for me to understand them. In fact, most of my friends and the people I'm closest to are also autistic and have similar experiences in terms of bullying and misunderstanding in the education system. Because of that, I tend to feel far closer to these people than to a neurotypical person who hadn't experienced these things.

For some of us, it's a shared trauma that's associated with our schooling experience, and we tend to gravitate towards each other to feel comfortable with people we understand better. My high school experience has been a lot different than my elementary school experience. For most of high school, I was in online learning, I didn't make any connections to people, and I spent most of my time in my room. Along with my social difficulties, this furthered my disconnect from people, specifically neuro-typical people. Making friends with anyone became difficult as I wasn't getting the experience. I also found it extremely difficult to do well in online schooling, as asking questions was far more difficult, and I didn't get any specialized learning tools or an EA to help me with my schooling. I find I tend to misunderstand instructions, and this was only exacer-bated further through online school, as if I misunderstood, there was no one around to tell me that I was doing it wrong. Until I inevitably handed in something that was not what was expected, I performed horribly and ultimately averaged a 60%.

Being Too Trusting in a Cynical World
By Brianna Longhenry

My mom really helped me start advocating for myself and is my number one cheerleader/supporter. I started volunteering at our local food bank so I could get one-on-one social experience. I started practicing and role playing with my mom at home, trying to understand different social cues. That September, I started I high school, and it was a big struggle, but I put in the hard work and time. I enrolled in a special class in my school for job placement and skill development. I did a few co-ops at two clothing stores in the mall, and even got hired with American Eagle.

I always had friendships, and, right up until grade 9, I was popular, with several very close friends. I never understood and still don't understand basic sarcasm and still will think people are serious when they are just joking around. I take so much offensively even today. Once I started high school, I had severe anxiety with things like going to the mall without my parents or going to parties, as I was never a rule breaker, I was never in trouble growing up, I always wanted to do right. I also think so many friends were intimidated with how close I was with my mom as well; she has always been my best friend, and, to other teens my age, that was odd to them.

I was active in sports in school. I played basketball, played on the senior volleyball team, and I was on the Ontario under 18 boxing team and would compete around Ontario. I think that is why most people were shocked to know that I had autism. One thing I always hear is, **"You don't seem or look autistic."** There are a few preconceptions about how I'm supposed to look, as well as what an autistic person is and is not capable of.

As someone with autism I trust too easily, and I expect everyone to be loyal and honest like I am. Unfortunately, that has gotten me into situations that has made me make mistakes at a young age. Like becoming pregnant at the age of 20. Just like I have embraced my autism I have embraced being the most amazing mom I can be, and I'm very proud of how far I have come and how great of a mom I am to my son.

Having autism as an adult is very hard. As soon as anyone knows you're autistic, they look at you differently, like you have this disease or uncurable medical issue. I struggle to this day to find a career and for even my family members to really understand what autism is and how my brain works.

I struggle with relationships, either romantic relationships or partnership. As I trust too easily, I allow people to get away with so much because they use my autism as their excuse to get away with abusive, controlling, behaviours. I'm the most forgiving and loyal person, and I expect everyone to be that way, but, unfortunately, they are not. I think one of the best things about having autism is that everyone I know that is autistic is very genuine, trustworthy, honest, and loyal. I also find as soon as someone hears that I have autism, they no longer have any interest.

PART 5: CREATIVITY

Meeting About Creativity—Dialogue

WE TALKED
EXPRESSIVENESS
AUTISTIC PERSPECTIVES ON ART, MUSIC, WRITING, AND THE DRIVE TO CREATE

SCOTT: In terms of creativity, I don't necessarily know that it has anything to do with autism, but I have always been creative and made stories. And even in my sleep, I have dreams, and I write them down, and sometimes they're stories. I can't say I've heard of anybody else who can do their job in their sleep. I've always drawn, and I've always written, since at least grade nine. I have a life drawing from grade nine that I did, and I still keep it. The one reason I like my job is it allows me to be creative in my head while working, and then I go home and write it down and draw out stories.

I work in a factory that makes car parts. So, I wrote an illustrated children's story about parts and how they get lost from the assembly line and have to find their way back a little bit. Akosua describes it as a mix of *Toy Story* and *WALL-E*, but I don't usually think of comparing it to other's stories. I tend to ignore a lot of media because it can be too distracting, and I want to focus on my own stuff.

AKOSUA: It is fascinating that you enjoy your work because it helps your creativity.

SCOTT: The story I'm writing on right now arose more than 25 years ago from another writing group I was in. We created a shared fictional universe and wrote stories, and now I'm using that universe again.

AKOSUA: Very cool. And so, how about you, Elliot? You play an instrument, don't you?

ELLIOT: I have played the bass guitar since I was 5 years old up. But, I've not only been creative with my bass guitar, but I've also been creative with arts and crafts, and I've also been creative with building

AKOSUA: And how do you feel when you're being creative?

ELLIOT: It makes me feel less stressed and more confident, as I'm building better fine motor skills with my disability and my autism as well too. Makes me feel better, and I use the music on my phone to calm myself down or listen to my buds.

DEBBIE [Elliot's mom]: He's got three guitars. Sometimes we go to the movies and he'll come home, and he's got three guitars. He'll just pick it up, and he can play after hearing a song once.

KATHERINE: By ear? Me too. I never learned how to read sheet music or tabs. And I think that was honestly a good thing, because I can learn anything just by ear.

DEBBIE: That's amazing.

SCOTT: Yeah. Music and art run in my family. So, I've always been able to remember music. My mom and her two sisters were professional singers.

[…]

BRIANNA: Listening to inspiring music helps me think creatively and it also helps me stay level-headed.

AKOSUA: And Corey, your stories are quite amazing. Do you want to talk a bit about your writing?

COREY: I really enjoy creating stories and I like being surprised by stories 'cuz there aren't a lot of original stories out there anymore. So when I come across something that truly catches me by surprise, I enjoy it.

AKOSUA: I'm going to get the group going again. We can still do that. And so Eric, You're a poet. I loved your poem. You did that for school. Was it the one that we've got in the compilation?

ERIC: Yes, it was a final assignment for one of my English classes. I mean sometimes I do poetry, sometimes short stories, but mostly my creative energy is spent on essays and stuff.

WAYMAN: I enjoy writing, and it's been a part of my long-term studies of certain things. A way of dealing with connectivity and things like that.

KATHERINE: I don't know who exactly said this quote first, but art's purpose is to disturb the comfortable and comfort the disturbed. And I wouldn't say, as someone with autism, that I'm personally disturbed or that is a common throughline. But I think there's an intrinsic weirdness to a lot of us. And I think when we create art, a lot of the time, it is for the purpose of expressing that. And I think if I didn't have my weirdness, I don't think I would like the art that I created.

AKOSUA: That definitely is a way of being creative. And Corey, you're master of that! You're always making us laugh.

COREY: Yeah, I agree with Katherine about art being a way of expressing the weirdness and the chaos in the head. When writing stories or reading the stories, I find the ones that tend to be the most chaotic, weird, and sometimes disturbed are the more enjoyable ones. Art that just makes you wonder what you're listening to or you're reading or you're watching. It's like, what the heck is this? They're the most interesting.

KATHERINE: Yeah. Another thing I would say is I think also a common theme with a lot of people with autism is that if they become extremely interested in something like a special interest, we will just absolutely hammer that home. We will get as good as possible at that or we will learn as much as possible with that. And I think with art that is one of the primary examples of that myself with music. I never used to write lyrics. I could write, but it was a different part of my brain than I was using when I write prose. It's a bit more logical. And then I decided that I really wanted to write lyrics. So, I have three or four thesauruses in my room and dictionaries and stuff, and I've focused in on that because I wanted to get better at that. That became my special interest and I think that desire to focus typically helps us a lot when it comes to art or creating or anything of the sort.

AKOSUA: So beautifully expressed.

Virtual Nightmare
By Corey Kearns

I came across this subway simulator a few years back, and I gotta say it was an interesting experience. There were a wide range of characters, such as an ice cream cone named Waffles and a subway conductor named Enzo. There were a bunch of other characters too like a leopard, a food cart, a talking gun and even a cowboy hat. I chose the ice cream cone, booted up the game, and found that it had a ton of settings. There was murder mystery, king of the train, subway shootout, and race against the conductor. I chose king of the train and found myself at the back of the train.

The cowboy hat showed up out of nowhere and offered to show me around. I accepted their offer because they seemed friendly but, all of a sudden, I hear the click of a revolver behind my head and on instinct I duck. It was then that I realized this was a free for all and anything was fair game. I tried to grab the gun from the cowboy hat, but, as I did that, sneaky hat pulled the trigger. The bullet got lodged in my creamy ice cream body, but, for some reason it didn't hurt a bit. I was holding my breath without realizing it but as I exhaled the bullet flew straight back into the revolvers chamber causing it to explode taking the cowboy with it.

I doubled over as my health went down and a message popped up saying Waffles triggers special ability: Ice Cream Shield. While I was trying to recover, the conductor and leopard came crashing into the room. They were battling it out like ninjas in a martial arts movie when the food cart rolled up beside me and offered me some popcorn. It smelled, amazing, and, despite myself, I couldn't help taking some. I also smelled almonds which was weird. Lucky for me the leopard performed a round-house kick at the wrong time, causing them to kick the popcorn out of my hands instead of launching the conductor out the window. The food cart cursed about wasted cyanide and started firing scolding hot drinks and sticky condiments at everyone. I ducked behind a seat just in time as the leopard got coated in sticky sauces and cooked to a fine crisp by the scalding liquids. The subway car smelled heavenly, but I knew it was a trap because the conductor who had evaded the attack fell into it. The conductor keeled over frothing at the mouth before his skin turned purple and his head exploded.

I booked it down the train car into the next as a stray bullet fired across the car I entered. The bullet missed me by an inch and hit the food cart with a thundering sound as a lightning bolt shot through the roof and fried the cart to a crisp. Now, it was just me and the gun, and it was anyone's game. The gun bowed his head and introduced himself, My name is Skippy Von Lightning Shots, I killed your attacker now prepare to fry." Skippy fired shot after shot as I dove and weaved through chairs and poles.

Lightning struck at the place every shot connected, which gave me an idea. I raced toward Skippy and dove on top of him engulfing him in my sweet and gooey ice cream centre. Skippy fired his final shot as lightning rang from the heavens, zapping us both frying Skippy to the core. My ice cream body exploded, and my cone base cracked, but I survived as big shiny neon letters popped on the screen, "Waffles wins King of The Train." The train car faded to black as I removed the VR helmet breathing rapidly from the experience. I looked around me seeing, a bunch of other players removing their helmets as well, smiling. They all approached me offering their hands in congratulations, introducing themselves before asking if I wanted to try another game. I smiled, nodded and slipped the helmet on for round 2. And that is how I became Waffles the Ice Cream Cone champion of the virtual world…

Dark Premonition
By Corey Kearns

One particularly eerie and stormy night under the light of a full moon, an abandoned snowmobile falls through the ice into Lake Ontario.

A crack leading straight to a series of tunnels that lead to earth's core resides near where the snowmobile lands at the bottom of the lake, and a surge of energy from the earth's core causes the snowmobile to undergo a supernatural transformation.

The snowmobile's tracks turn to blades, its steering wheel turns to a high-tech supercomputer, and it gains the ability to drive in any direction, but the most terrifying part is that this snowmobile becomes sentient.

The next day, after the storm had calmed, the individual who left the snowmobile on the ice returned to retrieve it only to be met with a most terrifying sight: a metal-made-flesh weremobile.

The individual falls to its knees begging forgiveness and the weremobile responded by decapitating them and then sewing their head on its dashboard.

The owner of the snowmobile wakes up to find that they are only a passenger in this now monstrous vehicle's life and are forced to watch as the weremobile parties, kills, and bargains its way to riches and power.

Now unrealistically wealthy, well connected, and admired, the weremobile parks itself in its 100-story penthouse for a well needed rest only to be assassinated by government agents and its assets seized.

The owner of the were-mobile wakes up with a fully intact body and realizes it was just a dream until they hear the dragging of track blades and the revving of unnatural sounding snowmobile engines. Lights flicker on, and the weremobile from the dreams begins speeding across the room, track blades raised and impales the owner through their chest.

As blood pours from their mouth, their life flashes before their eyes, and they realize they never owned a snowmobile.

The Final Curtain
By Corey Kearns

It was a cold winter afternoon, and Acedia Fires was chilling on a bench at her favourite petting zoo. She was writing her latest song, and she found winter to be the most inspiring time of year. She loved the melancholy in the scenery and how that snowy terrain added that little bit of beauty to the otherwise dying parts of nature. She loved how most of the animals hid and huddled together for warmth, and the world prepared to start anew when the new year rolled in.

Acedia Fires had a secret that she hadn't even shared with her family, you see, she was dying from an incurable illness. She wasn't scared of the end, nor was she ill prepared for the reaper's song. She just wanted to live as much as she could until her final breath, and her way of doing that was through song.

Acedia Fires stood up from the park bench and took a walk, enjoying the dead quiet of the petting zoo. She admired how, even as they lost their leaves and dried up in the cold, the trees stood strong as ever. She took the scenic route to her studio as she finished writing her final song. She was ready for her final curtain, but, as she entered her studio, she fell and was knocked unconscious.

Acedia Fires awoke in the hospital to her daughter and son sitting by her bedside crying. She placed her hands on their shoulders and told them there's no need for their tears. She told them she had lived a good life, and she had something she wished to pass onto them. Acedia Fires reached into her pocket and handed her children her last song and asked if they would sing it together for her.

Acedia Fires's children nodded and started rehearsing their mother's song with her together. When it came time for the show, she told them that they were ready to sing without her, but she would be in the audience cheering for them. The children got on stage and sang their hearts out to the song they practiced with their mum. A song titled "The Beauty in the Darkness."

Acedia Fires was the only one who could see it, but a cloaked figure sat next to her and listened to her children sing with her before standing and offering its hand. Acedia Fires accepted their hand and exited the theatre side by side with death. She smiled and thanked them for letting her have that final moment and passed on to the other side.

Death of the Universe
By Corey Kearns

Once upon a time, there was a robot surfer named Jerry who was tasked with watching over the flow of time. Jerry spent his days surfing the time-space continuum on his magic surfboard, visiting different times and just chilling. The problem with all of this was his visits weren't on purpose but complete accidents. You see, Jerry was very accident prone: one little trip here, and accidental beheading there, and, sometimes, he even accidentally destroyed a whole timeline. Jerry didn't seem to care, because he didn't have a care in the world until, one day he destroyed a timeline and suddenly there were no more time waves to ride. Jerry went to the masters of the universe to warn them, just to discover they were nothing but bones. Jerry found a note on the table addressed to him.

> To Jerry,
>
> If you're reading this that means you have probably killed us by accident. Why we decided to put someone like you in charge of the universe we will never know, but there is a way to salvage things: you must go to the center of the table and slam your board into the slot.
>
> P.S. Pls don't break the board, Jerry.
>
> The Masters

Jerry did as he was asked, but being Jerry has its disadvantages, and, by that, I mean yep, Jerry broke the magic board. The universe swirled to life and the masters reappeared and Jerry was confused. "How?" Jerry asked. "I broke the board."

The masters shrugged. "Jerry, we knew you would, but we also knew you might not if you thought it would be how things were to be fixed."

Jerry stared. "Do you think I wouldn't go through with it?"

The masters shook their heads. "No, but we know your luck."

Jerry shrugged. "Fair enough." and tripped over the plug to the universe's power source destroying himself and all life in the universe, because they are all robots by nature and without power they die.

And that is the story about how Jerry destroyed the universe

Mad Libs for Sports
By Elliot Smith

Rugby is a ______game. You have to ____the rugby ball _____to do
      Adjective   Verb   Adverb

a complete pass. You have to stay _____in order to get an assist, or
      Adverb

________________to score a try to get your __________. Whether
Verb Ending in "ing"   Favourite Food

you're winning or ________, you have learned how to ______support
       Silly Word   Adjective

you team with _______through a good ____or bad _________to
     Celebrity   Noun   Person in room

have a great group of ______
      Animals

In order to have a _____________coach. Rugby teaches
     Adjective with a/an

_____________to have a positive ________from __________to
Celebrity in Sports   Proper Noun   Favourite Movie

_____________so shooting the boot in ____________to treat the
Piece of Technology   Country in the World

_______like a family so they can from celebrate from
Silly Word

_____________to making sure that ____or _______can _____
Verb Ending in "ing"   Noun Best Friend   Adverb

learn about what happens at the _____stays at the ____. No matter
      Event   Noun

turnovers, _____________kicks, lineouts, or if you are giving back to
    Fruit or Vegetable

the ____community, you will be ______like a family!
  Noun   Adverb

An Ode to the Disabled
By Eric Lauder

Before you read, a simple note: this is a slightly altered poem that I previously wrote as an assignment for an English class during my undergraduate studies. It is a satirical poem, aiming to bring attention to the many issues faced by those with ASD, including from certain political figures and within institutions such as schools, and to mock those who perpetuate these issues. It should stand as an example of how I used my disability as a tool to inform my studies, granting me knowledge and insight to tackle issues other students might not consider, as well as a memoir discussing some issues that I faced. With that said, please enjoy.

An Ode to the Disabled
Oh, all you Disabled folk, this one's for thee.
We're done, we're through, as all can'st see.
At best, invisible, society's ills at worst,
Our needs are put anywhere but first,
And we stand in this corner, heads down, forgotten!
And who should stand, hands full of goods misbegotten,
But our illustrious Premier, shrugging off any naysay,
Lining his own fat pockets, he would'st simply say:
"Sticks and stones may break my bones,
But words won't hurt me," tripping over his own.
Yet were his intellect half as sharp as his shoes,
He'd likely split his whole mouth in two!
I would say the man's greed and vanity will be his undoing;
Yet, it seems it'll be ours, God above willing!
What's greed but a sin, anyways? What's Hell but hot?
I came here begging, praying to Him for help, but all I got
Was a fine "How do you do?" followed by dead silence.
"Not Well!" I shout, for ignorance is worse than violence,
Because at least then, you'd be looking me in the eye!
Why, to merely be noticed would show you had tried.

So, I sit again in silence. If the Almighty himself remains deaf
To my heartfelt pleas against our agonizingly slow death
What hope do I have of convincing the earless sinner in power
To change his mind during his (and our) darkest hour!
Yet, hideous as it may be, his face is just a face
For the bastardous creature we call the human race!
Where to start? At which vile tendril shall we begin?
How's about our glorious University, where within
Administrative process is so terribly, terribly foolish?
To have a chance, no shortage of long and boorish
Meetings must be sat through; and come back next year
To do it all over again! The issue, as you'll see here,
Is that a disabled full-time student surely has naught better to do
Than to drown in a sea of meetings I can't possibly swim through;
All to confirm that my disability hasn't up and walked off
Because, just as crippled legs will heal after long enough,
So, too, does my brain face the threat of becoming "normal."
I beg of thee, discard this stupid need to be formal.
The way I walk, talk, socialize, or better yet, thy past records
Should be ample proof that I am what I am, yet thine accords
Fail to stop thee from making my life a living hell!
In fact, from where I stand, 'tis almost like, well,
Like thou dost it on purpose merely to spite me!
To punish me for the sin of being unlike thee.
And what of our illustrious teachers, some of whom possess
Minds about as bright and spotless as a common beggar's dress.
Damn "group participation," or whatever thou may'st call it
Judging a man's worth based on his mouth rather than wit
And let anyone who says otherwise be promptly hung!
Because, as everyone knows, knowledge is stored in the tongue
While we parade around our heads, a motley cage of bone
Which only echoes, whispers, and ego call their own.
After all, what is something like crippling anxiety, here?
Just some illness none can see, let alone hear.
By all means, cling to the past like some ancient miser,
And you'll find that neither of us are any the wiser!
So go ahead! Dock my marks! I've no use for them now;
You aren't the first who's judged me as second-rate, anyhow.

Killer Santa
By Justin Humphreys

It was the night before Christmas, all was silent, not a sound through the house. Someone left the 12 days of Christmas fruit out knowing that Santa would go for it. He took a bite and quickly realized he shouldn't have been so greedy. Santa passes out and dies shortly after a spell that poisoned the fruit.

The children come downstairs the next morning to see their dad bringing Santa back with a forbidden spell in the kitchen. But the spell has side effects. Now Santa's a killer, and he kills the boys and girls on the naughty list year after year, naughty children beware. Your parents can't protect you from Santa. With that, he's the cause of houses haunted by the victims of Santa all over the world—including the house I'm in right now.

Now it's time to tell you Santa's backstory: Santa's parents fled England during the witch trials due to them being a witch and wizard. This means Santa is a wizard. Santa's grandparents moved with his parents to the North Pole, moving for the second time. The first time Santa's grandparents moved it was for better employment opportunities and they moved, from Germany. That's why Santa's last name is "Claus."

Santa had jobs before he delivered gifts. For a time, he owned his own bakery. That's how he was first introduced to cookies. He then owned a bar/restaurant. That's where he met Mrs. Claus. He also worked at a clothing store and, for a short time, at a publishing company, but he wasn't happy with most of these jobs, though he loved working at the bakery and bar/restaurant.

Now that Santa is evil, this year, he took it further. He gave out the launch codes for the nukes alongside toys to all the children in the USA. One of the children accidentally launched a nuke into Russia, starting WW3, so the wizarding world law enforcement was after Santa. They sent Santa's famous family member, that one with a lightning scar on his forehead, his great-great nephew, to help out. They found out that Santa was asked by a politician to give out the launch codes for the nukes.

In the chaos, the reindeer were killed after Santa's evilness was discovered. A spell turned them into flesh-eating reindeer. Now Santa and the reindeer have to kill and fly. They can't help it. Only the magic of his great-great nephew stops the killing, or it would be worse every Christmas.

Children that Santa doesn't kill are sometimes kidnapped and fed to the reindeer. This was the final indignity. His great-great nephew was forced to kill Santa with a forbidden spell. This means an end to his reign of terror, but there will be no more Christmases either.

Pizza Hut Killer
By Justin Humphreys

It was stormy weather outside when the Pizza Hut killer began his killing spree. It started at a gas station. He killed an entire family, and their pet baby donkey, then moved on to murders in Pizza Huts all over the USA and Canada. At every crime scene he would troll the police. One of the things he did to troll the police was to send them to the house of actor Mike Myers and leave clues to make them believe he was the killer.

Thirty years have gone by; the police still can't solve the murders. After the police stopped looking at Mike Myers as a suspect, the killer had police suspecting all of Hollywood. Every actor and actress in Hollywood was under investigation by the police. The police were busy questioning every actor and actress in Hollywood while the sprees kept happening.

O Brian's vs Shykarens
By Justin Humphreys

Once upon a time, there was a family that could see that invisible creatures named shykarens that were invisible to the average person. They hunted shykarens to keep humanity safe. They would behead shykarens and burn their remains, until Brian, one of the sons of the family, fell for a shykaren named Rachel. They ran away together knowing that their families wouldn't accept their love for each other.

Years went by, and they got married, then they decided to start a family of their own. Their families found out about their relationship and marriage. They weren't happy. Rachel's family wanted to kick her out of the family, and Brian's family was about to behead Rachel until her family found out that they were grandparents and told them. So, they didn't kill Rachel, but they continue to hunt down the shykarens that are a threat to humanity and behead them one by one to keep the world safe.

Rachel's family cries whenever a shykaren is killed, and Brian's family celebrates. Even though they each look different, Rachel and Brian's children are shykarens. They look like an eagle/human hybrid because Brian's family are human. Rachel's kids have human faces and talons with knuckles for hands, human legs, and talons for feet. They have a beak for a mouth and wings on their backs. They also have feathers.

After finding out they were all going to be grandparents, the Shykarens stopped fighting to behead Rachel. They wanted to celebrate and forget about each other's actions in the past. Brian's dad got out joints an, Rachel's dad got out a bottle of alcohol. Both Brian's dad and Rachel's dad start fighting again when they see what the other brought out to celebrate. They decided instead to go to Las Vegas, which didn't go well when their wives found out about their trip. As soon as they were found out, both Brian's and Rachel's dads resolved the problem by inviting their wives and the rest of the family with them.

All of them had fun in Vegas. They got kicked out of all of the casinos, one after the other, for winning too much money.

Sometimes
By Wayman Edward Sole

- Sometimes I get angry.
- Sometimes I get FRUSTRATED.

What happens then?

I get confused.

- I cannot find the words I want to say.
- I lose track of what I'm doing.
- My mind gets stuck on one thing.

What do I do?

I get angry - but my anger does NOT help.

- I get frustrated - but my frustration does NOT help.

But Frustration and Anger

Make me anxious.

- Causes tension
- Causes negative feelings

HOW CAN I HELP MYSELF?

I can always:

- Close my eyes to block things I see that distract or confuse me;

- Stop listening to block things I hear that distract or confuse me;
- Always relax until all my tension falls away from me.

When I am relaxed

It is easier for me to understand the things I see;

- It is easier for me to understand the things I hear;
- It is easier for me to keep track of what I'm doing;
- It is easier for me to be me.

Autism is Me Every Day
By Justin Milner

Autism is a great character. They come out of nowhere and stay for as long as you want. It's warm, smooth, touchless almost like a feeling. It carries a bag of happiness and amazement. It whispers that it was amazing.

Toronto Islands

Autism is unique, accomplishing so much every day. Autism is funny and makes you laugh so hard. Autism is kind of weird in its own way. Autism is me, it makes me every day, motivates me, makes me smile, and makes me human.

Ripley's Aquarium

A true friend doesn't care if you're rich or poor, if you're being an ass, what you weigh, what you look like, what car you drive, where you live, or if you have a family or not. Your conversations will always start where you left off, even if weeks go by. They will be there for you when you need them the most and, regardless of your faults, they will always love you and stand by at your best and worst times. That's a true friend to me!

Toronto Blue Jays

Toronto Blue Jays game from Rogers Center Toronto, 2022, when I caught a game winning Baseball.

I am crazy and hilarious. I wonder how things fall into place. I hear violence and sadness; I see the beauty of the world. I want to be free.

I am crazy and hilarious. I pretend everything is perfect when it is not. I feel the wind and sun. I touch my soul. I worry about other people and not myself. I cry at the hatred.

I am crazy and hilarious. I understand as much as I can, I say nothing, I dream every day and live it, I try everything and do everything, I hope for a better future.

I am crazy and hilarious.

I am a beautiful soul, inside and out—like a warm summer day, a happy song you will never forget. A breath of fresh air and treats of fresh water. I am great all around: smell, touch, hear, perfect to look at.

Algonquin Park Truck & Trial

It was the summer of 2018, and I was on a camping adventure at Algonquin Park. I remember the trip like it was yesterday and there was a beautiful hiking trail that caught my eye. It was estimated the hike would take eight hours, and I was ready for it. It was so peaceful and quiet—I was the only one on the trail, one with nature. Halfway through the hike, the black flies were getting really bad, and, of course, I ran out of bug spray. I was whipping my arms and legs around to shake them off. I could feel the bumps, and my towel was covered in blood and sweat. I was determined to make it on top of the mountain side, as I knew it would be the most awesome sight I've even seen.

When I made it to the top, all I could do was to just sit. It was astonishingly beautiful. The wind felt good; it was just amazing to look out and see as far I could see. I sat on the rock and said, "I need a picture." As the evening drew to a close, I never wanted this to end. I wish I could stay up for just a little while longer. Then I wandered around for hours unable to find my way back. I knew it would be dark soon, and I had to get back.

It started to rain and thunderstorm; I took cover in a nearby cave. Venturing further down the cave, I decided to sit and wait for the rain to pass. The rain had stopped but I could still hear water, so I took a few more steps, and there it was—a big waterfall, the most amazing sight. The ground started to shift. Suddenly I was headed right into the water below, at the foot of the falls.

I must have been washed up the river at least 50 miles away. Then, a shipwreck appeared out of nowhere, as I climbed on to dry land. I was really confused. I closed my eyes, and I could see daylight. I opened my eyes, and saw I was in my tent! How much of what happened was a dream? I don't know. All I knew was I had so much fun.

Journey Behind the Falls

Whose Stories?
By Justin Humphreys

A lone fisherman was out on his boat late at night. As fish started to come up to his line. All the sudden, something hits the side of the boat, causing it to rock back and forth and then silence. A man emerged from the waters, as the fisherman shined a light on him. He had no face, just a hood and a hook for a hand. The man fell back into the water, just the hood left behind.

One day, James is walking down the street, and he saw a lady talking to herself. He thought to himself, *I wonder what her story is.* As James sat on a park bench waiting for his friend to meet up for lunch, he watched the woman laughing and having a good time with herself. It was the most bizarre thing he had ever seen. He laughed too. The friend finally got to the bench and was perplexed. He asked James what was so funny, and James pointed and explained. His friend was stunned. The friend said, "I think you are crazy. There is no one there."

Steve has been attending anger management classes for the past two months. He feels he doesn't have an anger issue—he just likes to make dolls of people he doesn't like and throw them off the water tower. Steve feels that he could be a better person if he took the classes, so he took them. Now he doesn't throw anything off the tower. Instead, he calls people and torments them. Maybe a few more classes and months of anger management will be good for him. Steve personally thinks everyone else is nuts, although they all think he's the one who is nuts.

Brad was camping up north on Ellesmere Island, on top of a snow-covered mountain overlooking the Atlantic Ocean. It was mid-April, so it was cold when he decided to venture into the town of Alert, the most northern town in the world. As he was walking, he realized a polar bear was following him. He started running, but the bear was still too close. He stopped and the bear stopped, too. Brad ran into a coffee shop. The bear followed him in. As the worker ran to the door a throw coffee into the snow, the bear left and started eating the coffee-flavoured snow. It was a story for the ages for Brad, as at least the bear stopped following him.

After finishing college, Harry needed to find a place to live. Everywhere was too expensive, and, with the price of gas, this was a bit of a challenge. After weeks of looking, Harry decided to live in an RV to have the van life. He figured it would be so cool to cut down on rent and other expenses. Looking online, he finally found the perfect van. When Harry bought it, he was so happy: one bed, a kitchen, and a small bathroom with a shower. The only problem was finding parking every night, but it was worth it. Five years later, he saved so much money and the travelling has not stopped.

Once upon a time, there was a sushi restaurant on a mountain in Japan. It was haunted by an employee that was murdered. His ghost is said to be haunting the restaurant, looking for revenge. One day, an actor, Ryan Johnson, walked into the restaurant. He was unaware that he was related to the person who murdered the employee in the 1950s. The murderer was his grandfather, Jeffrey Johnson.

After dinner, he went to the washroom and was murdered by the ghost. Tokyo police found his dismembered body. They started an investigation. When they found out about the ghost seeking revenge, they were convinced it was the ghost who killed the actor. Tokyo police closed the investigation, upsetting Ryan's family. Upon hearing the news, his family was grieving. His mother looked over to his grandfather and heard him say, "Damn you, Toezoko Wannabe!"

He knew the of name of the ghost from the sushi restaurant his grandson died in. She comforted him and he told her the story of the ghost. "I knew a man once," he said. "Toezoko Wannabe. He worked at a sushi restaurant on a mountain, as I was a bank robber on the run. One day, he found out and was going to turn me in, so I murdered him."

His grandfather cried as he told the story. When he was done crying, he said, "Toezoko was my friend, and I couldn't go to prison with a daughter to take care of and a wife back home." He explained. Toezoko's ghost murder of Ryan was revenge for he did. Then he saw Toezoko's ghost—it appeared before them. The ghost said, "You should've told me about your wife and baby girl, I forgive you, my friend."

Shortly after this, Toezoko's ghost disappeared from the restaurant. Now standing in front of him the old man was his grandson's ghost. The old man said, "Ryan you're here!"

Ryan said, "Yes, and I heard everything. I was murdered because of your actions. Toezoko had a family of his own. A son and wife who never had the chance to celebrate birthdays with him. He never gets to meet his grandchildren—all because of you!" Then Ryan disappeared, disappointed and disgusted with his grandfather.

As Ryan's family grieved, Toezoko's family got answers from Ryan's ghost. Toezoko's family forgave Ryan's grandfather for his actions. After Ryan's funeral, his grandfather turned himself in for Toczoko's murdcr. Now Toezoko's spirit is at rest, and Ryan's grandfather is in prison for murder. Ryan's family is crying even more knowing that they will never again see his grandfather out of prison. Two families were destroyed due to the actions of Ryan's grandfather.

Art by Scott R. Dawson

Scott R. Dawson drawings -
the incredible frog boy, half boy half frog leaps into the air

Scott R. Dawson drawings -
rat crossing the road

Scott R. Dawson drawings -
buying a ticket for a show

Scott R. Dawson drawings -
scaffolding with desk and writer on top backlit by a full moon

Scott R. Dawson drawings -
giant fishman chasing a bird

Scott R. Dawson drawings -
a large woman staring at an elephant posed at the tip of her index finger

I Am ... We Are
By Elliot Smith

I am…………..me,
Can't you see?
I want to be free—
What a world this could be.

Takiwatanga is the Maori word,
If you have not heard.
It means in your own space and time,
No mountain is too small to climb.

Autism is a strategy,
Not a tragedy,
We may think differently,
But don't give us sympathy.

We are not different or less,
I must confess,
We are the same,
No more room to blame.

We want to be seen,
Please don't be mean.
Include us all the time,
It won't cost you a dime.
It's all about acceptance and inclusion,
Let's advocate for a solution,
If we work together as a team,
We can believe in ourselves to reach our dream.

Bios

Akosua Joy Brown

Akosua is the editor and compiler of this book, and, while she is "neuro-spicy," she is an "autism mom," and is not autistic herself. She loves to help people get the best version of their stories out in the world—published as a legacy book. She has helped hundreds of writers hit their goal to be published authors. She is a mom to four, and all are neuro-diverse. Her journey to support autistic kids let to her creating Outfox Magazine—a magazine which celebrated, educated, inspired diversity and acceptance. The team published 20 issues before folding during the COVID-19 pandemic. She then created Creative Expressions, a meeting for autistic adults where we explored our creativity, writing short stories, poems, and scripts which we then performed.

She founded What's Your Story—Author Services and continues to run writing programs which enable all to publish the books of their dreams. She lives with her children, three cats, and a dog in Hamilton, Ontario, Canada. She loves to write, crochet, quilt, and longs for a home near a beach.

One day!

Owen Bryan

The real person behind this pseudonym is a 29-year-old entrepreneur about to start a business doing digital marketing. He is the eldest sibling of four and is great at fixing cars and pretty much anything with an engine. In the midst of this seasons' "polar vortex," he fixed an old but economical-to-run baseboard heater and kept his family warm. He is also great with the innards of computers. He is quite good at problem solving on many levels.

Although he is often down due to life circumstances, he also has ambitions to make a lot of money and build his own house in a lovely spot in the woods. He is not sure which country the woods will be located in, but he is sure that they will be beautiful.

Scott R. Dawson

Scott Robert Dawson sometimes dreams about fictional worlds and has had story ideas while washing the dishes. Forty pages into a story, he discovered that he had no idea how to build a plot, which led him to study story design and screenwriting. Now he creates cartoons, and is writing, illustrating, and translating children's books, giving rise to a vast multilingual publishing empire. He listens to trance music and plays way too much Minecraft. Find out more about his work at srdbooks.ca.

Ciara Freeman

Howdy! I'm Ciara, I'm just a fun lovin' gamer girl from the UK, and I'm a night owl!

Justin Humphreys

Justin is looking for work as a chef if you are hiring! He lives near Bowmanville, Ontario, Canada and loves to make people laugh. He is a hunter, plays the guitar, and is a graduate of chef school.

Corey James Shawn Kearns

My Name is Corey James Shawn Kearns, and I am 29 years old. I am an avid gamer, a reader, writer, and artist. I love most types of games and stories, as well as trying new things. I am a witty, a joker, and a very free spirited person. My favourite food is spaghetti, my favourite dessert is Nanaimo bars, and my favourite drink is pop.

Eric Lauder

Eric is in his mid-twenties and will soon graduate from the University of Toronto. He helps his mom care for his two younger siblings, who are more impacted by autism than he is. Eric loves gaming and is a great cook.

Katie Layne

Hello, my name is Katherine Layne, I'm 18, I'm from Cobourg, Ontario, my pronouns are she/her, and I have been diagnosed with Asperger's Syndrome or High Functioning autism. My primary hobbies include writing (duh), playing instruments, such as piano, guitar, and esophagus, and I also do voice acting on the side for an indie animation project.

Also, I love my four cats.

Brianna Longhenry

Brianna Longhenry born in Oshawa, Ontario. Diagnosed with autism at age ten. First time participating in writing, although she was one of the ASD Superstars and Peer Support with *Outfox Magazine*. She wants to spread awareness about autism as she is a young adult trying to survive in a world that doesn't understand autism. When she is not reading a book, you can find her spending most of her time with family and her fur babies. Top thing on her bucket list is to be able to advocate through live speeches at schools spreading awareness about autism and explaining what invisible disabilities may and may not look like.

Lord Justin Milner

Lord Justin Milner - The man who lived a pretty interesting life. A simple man with autism living the dream one day at a time. He likes to think of himself as a adventurer always on the move and always busy. He says he is a boring person, but, in realty, he has been living a pretty interesting life. Very laid-back and always happy about something. He is in his thirties.

Elliot Gary Smith

My name is Elliot Gary Smith, and I am 25 years old. I was born in Wellington, New Zealand, at the Children's Hospital and now I live in Canada with my mom. I have dual citizenship, so I belong to New Zealand, and I belong to Canada.

I work part time as a Physical Fitness and Literacy Associate and a Mixed Ability Sports Facilitator. I live with my mother in an apartment, and I have two pets named Sandy (a lop rabbit, who is eight years old) and Casper (a Maine Coon Cat, who is four years old). I am very independent and go to the store for my mother, do laundry, and house chores, and I can take the bus by myself. I am interested in sharing my story in this book because I want to be a role model and show others that the sky's the limit, and nothing is impossible.

I am a children's book author and have written two books now with my mom called *Mateo's Mixed Ability Match* and *Elliot's Excellent MARI Match*. I am the Co-Captain of the Mixed Ability Rugby Team for the Oshawa Vikings and a World Cup Finalist. I have won many awards for my advocacy and volunteer work for the disability community. I am a proud committee member for the JaysCare Youth Advisory Committee, the Youth Advisory Committee for Grandview and for the Sport and Inclusion Team at the Abilities Centre.

WAYMAN EDWARD SOLE

Retired, a widower, and, by the time of publishing, wes will be 87 years old. He lives in London, Ontario, Canada and is a proud veteran and a grandfather who spent much of his career working on computers. He helped dyslexic children understand themselves and also developed ways to help nonverbal kids on the spectrum communicate using clay.

ROBERT WILLIAMS

A Reiki Master skilled at healing people over long distances, Robert is on a spiritual quest and creates peace and calm wherever he goes.

About Renaissance

Renaissance was founded in May 2013 by a group of authors and designers who wanted to publish and market those stories which don't always fit neatly in a genre, or a niche, or a demographic. Like the happy pan-bibliophiles we are, we opened our submissions, with no other guideline than finding a Canadian book we would fall in love with.

Today, this is still very true; however, we've also noticed an interesting trend in what we like to publish. It turns out that we are naturally drawn to the voices of those who are members of a marginalized group, and these are the voices we want to continue to uplift.

At Renaissance, we do things differently. We are passionate about books, and we care as much about our authors enjoying the publishing process as we do about our readers enjoying a great Canadian read on the platform they prefer.

pressesrenaissancepress.ca

pressesrenaissancepress@gmail.com

With great powerchair comes great responsibility…

It's a bird, it's a plane, it's… accessibility!

You wouldn't like me when I'm out of spoons…

All too often, superhero media depicts disability as something to overcome on the journey to becoming a hero, or as a sign of villainy. It's time to make heroism accessible for everyone.

In these 15 stories, you'll meet winged wheelchair users, supernatural spoonies, guardians with glaucoma, and many more. These disabled superheroes fight villains as well as outdated ableist stereotypes, and show that anyone can be Mighty.